"So then, you think me a silly young lady."

"Never silly. You, milady, are an enigma."

"An enigma?"

"That means you are—"

"I know what *enigma* means." He must think her a simpleton.

He chuckled. "I think you lean more toward being mysterious rather than difficult to understand."

She liked being mysterious.

"But I also find you enchanting and delightfully fascinating."

She liked the sound of those. A delightfully fascinating young lady who enchants.

"On the outside, you may appear ordinary, but on the inside, you are extraordinary, full of wit and charm and intelligence."

But did he think she was pretty?

MARY DAVIS

is an award-winning author of more than a dozen novels, both historical and contemporary, four novellas, two compilations and three short stories, as well as being included in various collections. She is a member of American Christian Fiction Writers and is active in two critique groups.

Mary lives in the Colorado Rocky Mountains with her husband of thirty years and three cats. She has three adult children and one grandchild. She enjoys board and card games, rain and cats. She would enjoy gardening if she didn't have a black thumb. Her hobbies are quilting, porcelain doll making, sewing, crafts, crocheting and knitting. Please visit her website at marydavisbooks.com.

MARY DAVIS

Her Honorable Enemy

HEARTSONG
PRESENTS

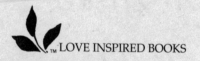LOVE INSPIRED BOOKS

Recycling programs
for this product may
not exist in your area.

ISBN-13: 978-0-373-48737-0

Her Honorable Enemy

Copyright © 2014 by Mary Davis

This edition published by arrangement with Love Inspired Books.

® and ™ are trademarks of Love Inspired Books, used under license.
Trademarks indicated with ® are registered in the United States Patent
and Trademark Office, the Canadian Intellectual Property Office and in
other countries.

www.Harlequin.com

Printed in U.S.A.

Honor thy father and thy mother:
that thy days may be long upon the land
which the Lord thy God giveth thee.
—*Exodus* 20:12

I dedicate this book in loving memory to my son Josh,
to Chip, my husband of thirty years,
and to my new grandbaby.

San Juan Islands Historical Note

The Pig War *was* a real event. The Oregon Treaty of 1846 drew a line at the 49th parallel. South of this dividing line belonged to America and north was British Columbia. There was an unsettled issue of the islands between Haro Strait and Rosario Strait. The treaty gave all of Vancouver Island to Great Britain even though it lay on both sides of the dividing line. The treaty was ambiguous on the islands that lay between Vancouver Island and the American coast. Both sides believed the San Juan Islands belonged to them.

In 1859, Lyman Cutlar, an American, shot and killed a British Hudson Bay Company pig over a matter of uprooted potatoes. With troops accumulating on both sides, the officers in charge agreed to hold dual occupancy of the islands until it was decided to which country they belonged. From 1859–1872 San Juan Island was occupied by both American and English troops. This was known as the Pig War, because the pig was the only casualty.

The American and the English officers got on quite well during the joint occupancy. The English held parties that they invited Americans to, and both sides held games and races in which everyone participated to alleviate the boredom of a war without much conflict.

William, Emperor of Germany, was chosen by both sides to arbitrate the San Juan case. On October 21, 1872, he decided that the San Juan Islands rightfully belonged to the United States of America.

Chapter 1

San Juan Island, Washington Territory,
Fall 1870

"'See, how she leans her cheek upon her hand! O, that I were a glove upon that hand, That I might touch that cheek!'"

Sitting against the woodpile, Rachel Thompson pressed the open book to her chest with one hand and put her other on her cheek. She closed her eyes and imagined the strong hand of a handsome man on her face. "Wherefore art thou *my* Romeo?"

"Rachel?" her stepmother called.

Rachel groaned. Could she just hide here and pretend she hadn't heard?

Honor thy father and thy mother.

Genevieve wasn't really her mother.

But if she disobeyed, Papa would find out somehow. She hated it when he gave her one of his disapproving looks. She pushed to her feet and slipped the book into her apron pocket.

Her half brother and half sisters were playing in the yard. Ages twelve, eleven, seven and five.

She stepped into the dim interior of the clapboard house. It was not large, but it had three bedrooms, a kitchen large enough for a dining table and a parlor with sliding pocket doors.

Her stepmother sat in a rocking chair, nursing the six-month-old baby, Priscilla. "Did you finish your chores?"

"Yes." Is that all she'd called her in here for?

"Have the children finished their chores?"

By the looks of them playing when she'd come in, she guessed not. "I don't know."

Priscilla finished nursing and sat up on her mama's lap.

Genevieve buttoned her shirtwaist and stood, settling Priscilla on her hip. She pulled the book out of Rachel's pocket and shook her head. "Rachel, dear, love is not like you read in your books. Romantic dreaming will not get you a husband. Love is hard work. You're twenty. You need to stop dreaming." She put the book on the fireplace mantel. "Would you make sure the children complete their chores?"

"Is it now my job to raise them?" She regretted her words the moment they crossed her lips. Genevieve had been a fine mother to her since she was seven.

"Of course not. But you are such a big help to me. And you know I appreciate you. When you get your head out of the clouds and find a husband, you won't have to bother with any of us. But until then, while you are under your father's roof, you will do your part."

Rachel wished she could throw a tantrum, but Genevieve was right. Her stepmother wasn't being unreasonable. And if Rachel complained to Papa, he would know she was being childish and treat her that way. "When the children's chores are completed, may I take a walk in the woods?"

"To dream, no doubt. I don't understand your affinity for the woods, but yes. Just don't be long. I'll need help this afternoon." Genevieve carried Priscilla upstairs to change her diaper.

Rachel took one step toward the door, turned, snagged her book from the mantel and dashed out.

The children had done only half their chores, if that. It wasn't that they *couldn't* finish them. It was that they knew they could get away with not doing them when their mama was busy with the baby. After all, none of them had chores half as hard as Rachel's. She dreaded trying to get all four of them to complete what little work they had. It could take her much of the day, having to watch them one at a time.

So she wouldn't. All her stepmother cared about was that the chores were done. How much faster it would be if she did them herself. So she made short work of them and then slipped off into the forest.

Knowing just where she wanted to sit and read, she patted her book in her apron pocket and trudged through the underbrush. The forest smelled so fresh, even though yesterday's rain had made everything wet. Her skirt got soaked in a hurry, but she didn't care. She was free to enjoy a good chunk of the day in peace.

Crackle.

She froze and then spun around. Was that an animal or a person? Studying the terrain and seeing nothing, she continued. When dead ground cover crunched behind her again, she kept walking until she could pinpoint the noise's precise location. Whatever was making it wasn't moving away.

It was tracking her.

So it wasn't likely an animal. At least not the four-legged variety.

Another step, and she swung around. She caught sight of the corner of a blue jacket.

"Lindy!"

Her twelve-year-old half brother, Lindley, stepped out from behind a large fir tree, not at all contrite at having been caught. With his hands shoved deep in his pants pockets, he swaggered up to her. "Where you goin', Rachel?"

She narrowed her eyes. "It is none of your concern. Now go home and play with the other children."

He shook his head. "But they're girls." He sounded indignant that she would even suggest such a thing.

"I'm a girl."

"But you don't do girl stuff and play with dolls." He shivered dramatically and eyed the forest behind her. "You're headed toward English Camp."

Heaven help her if he tattled that an American girl was walking where she shouldn't. Not with a war going on.

Lindley's expression turned to a triumphant smirk. "If you let me go with you, I won't tell no one."

If she didn't let him come, he would blackmail her. She'd wanted time to herself. She could just stop right where they were and read, boring him until he left. Better yet, she could read *Romeo and Juliet* aloud and scare him off. But he might wait at a distance and still follow. Of all her siblings, he could be the quietest. "Fine. You can come. But you have to do as I tell you."

He strode ahead. "Come on. What are you waiting for?"

She caught up and took the lead. "Stay quiet."

As she drew closer to the hill overlooking English Camp and Garrison Bay, she crouched and slowed. She had to make sure they stayed clear of the officers' quarters and that no guards were patrolling up here.

The soldiers were marching around the field down below on the other side of the fancy garden. The reason she liked to come. The garden, not the soldiers.

"Wow," Lindley said. "Look at all of them. How many do you think there are? Thousands?"

Rachel shifted her gaze from the blooming colors to the soldiers beyond and scoffed. "Hardly. The agreement between the American officers and the English officers was to hold dual occupancy of the islands until the matter of possession could be decided. Neither side is to have more than one hundred men. That was over ten years ago. You were too young to recall how it began." But she remembered the tension on the island at first. She'd been afraid Papa would have to go fight and be killed.

"And you think the no-good English will keep to that?"

"I've counted before. I never got more than seventy or eighty. A handful of men were likely inside the buildings or off somewhere else." She realized too late that her statements implied she'd been here several times. She hoped Lindley didn't make the connection. Or at least didn't make a fuss about it.

"Or maybe they are hiding a lot of soldiers in those buildings for a surprise attack, letting only a few out at a time so we don't know how many are really here. A conniving, scheming, cutthroat bunch, the English are."

Rachel rolled her eyes. He was repeating Papa's words to the letter. But she knew he secretly admired the soldiers on both sides. He was a boy, after all.

A dinner bell rang, and the soldiers marched off the field. The middle of the afternoon was a strange time to have a meal.

All became quiet down below.

After a few moments, Lindley scuttled down the side of the hill.

"Where are you going?" Rachel called after him.

"I want a better look."

"Get back here."

But he kept going.

She threw up her hands. What was she to do now? She couldn't let him go by himself. She shuffled her way down, at times sliding. If Papa found out, he would have both their hides. When she got to the bottom, Lindley was crouched behind a tree stump. She joined him. "What happened to doing as you were told?"

"No one's around." He stood and walked toward the manicured garden. "Come on."

The water in Garrison Bay lapped gently at the shore, the strong smell of salt wafted on the breeze, and nearby seagulls screeched.

The garden she had stared at all summer had short hedgerows around flower beds, all encircled by a white picket fence. Each bed had a different type of flower. She cautiously inched up to the garden. The flowers were lovely. She surveyed the camp and saw no one, so she opened the small gate at the end closest to her and eased it shut so as not to make any noise. She went from flower bed to flower bed, peonies, zinnias, daisies. The spring tulips and crocuses had long been replaced by summer and fall varieties.

As she was studying a yellow bloom she didn't recognize, she heard Lindley gasp and she spun around.

An English officer stood before her. A handsome officer with wavy brown hair. "May I help you, miss?"

She could see where Lindley crouched behind a low hedge, so she stepped back one pace, then another. And as she had hoped, the officer moved forward. Dare she speak? He would know for sure she wasn't English.

And was trespassing.

She wiggled her hand to get Lindley to run.

And run he did. But he let the gate swing shut behind him, making a tapping noise.

The officer turned and saw Lindley scampering for the hillside.

"Run, Lindy! Run!"

The officer stared at her with raised eyebrows. "American. What is your name?"

She might be captured, but she didn't have to speak. She pressed her lips together.

"Come now. You can tell me your name. I'm Leftenant Charles Young. And you are?"

Lef-tenant? She just loved the way the English spoke. Telling him her name couldn't really do any harm, but she held her tongue.

The *lef*tenant plucked a small purple flower from the nearby bed. "Were you enjoying our formal garden?" He held out the flower to her.

Rachel took it without thinking and smelled it. He wished to speak of the garden? What was he playing at?

He waited patiently for her to say something.

She twirled the flower.

A smile pulled at his mouth but didn't quite succeed. "What book are you reading?" He pointed at her apron.

She covered the pocketed book with one hand. He wouldn't take it from her, would he? He certainly was trying to start a conversation. As a captive of the enemy, she would not indulge him.

"Come now, I just want to know the title."

Pulling it out, she showed him.

"Shakespeare. Are you enjoying it?"

If she refused to answer any of his questions, maybe he would tire of this and let her be on her way.

He studied her, waiting, then said, "Maybe you can't

read at all and just carry a book around to look as though you can."

"I can so read. 'Two households, both alike in dignity, in fair Verona, where we lay our scene, from ancient grudge break to new mutiny, where civil blood makes civil hands unclean.'"

He smiled. A warm, inviting smile. "You can speak, other than to shout to the boy. 'From forth the fatal loins of these two foes a pair of star-cross'd lovers take their life; whose misadventured piteous overthrows do with their death bury their parents' strife.'"

This Englishman knew *Romeo and Juliet*?

Rachel continued the opening quotation. "'The fearful passage of their death-mark'd love, and the continuance of their parents' rage, which, but their children's end, nought could remove, is now the two hours' traffic of our stage…'"

"'The which if you with patient ears attend, what here shall miss, our toil shall strive to mend.'" He gave her a graceful bow with a flourish of his hand.

Her breath caught in her throat. He spoke the words so eloquently, as though Romeo himself were standing before her.

A soldier came up to the little white picket fence surrounding the garden. "Sir, tea is served in your office."

"Thank you. Would you bring another cup? I will be having a guest." The leftenant motioned to her. "Come this way."

Rachel glanced back and saw Lindley scrambling out of sight at the top of the hill. At least he had gotten away. She maneuvered through the garden and out the other side. Entering a long building, she saw several soldiers sipping their tea and was ushered into an office. Was this teatime?

He touched the back of a wooden chair. "Have a seat."

Was this where he would interrogate her? She thought

about refusing, to see what he would do, but chose to sit. What did he have planned for her?

"Now, your name?"

"Isn't it improper for a lady to introduce herself?"

Amusement danced in his gold-flecked hazel-brown eyes. "Not when there is no other to make her introductions."

"I have no name, so introductions are unnecessary." She paused. "Are you going to put me in your jail or the stockade?" She would rather be in jail than on display in the stockade. She swallowed hard. "Or am I to stand before the firing squad?"

Firing squad? Lieutenant Charles Young nearly choked on a laugh. This girl had quite a deep well for the dramatic. "I'm sorry, the firing squad is off duty at the moment. You will have to suffer my company."

How old was this raven-haired beauty with eyes the color of the ocean? Fifteen or sixteen? Her face was round, almost heart-shaped. When she came of age, she would so securely steal a man's heart, he would be helpless. Her every wish *his* command.

Nay, she would have a gaggle of boys falling over themselves to capture a morsel of her attention, hoping for a passing glance.

Under his scrutiny, she shifted in the chair. "If the death of a British pig could start this war, then imagine what will happen when they find out what the British have done with me."

Charles contained his smile. He would like to see her reaction to a little teasing. He leaned closer. "No one will ever know. We British are adept at disposing of bodies."

The girl gasped.

He did laugh then.

She couldn't possibly believe him. A gullible, melodramatic little thing. But how could anyone take a so-called war seriously when the only casualty was a pig shot ten years ago, starting it all? Since then, it had been a peaceful standoff.

He would ease her fears. "I promise you, milady, no harm will befall you whilst you are in my charge."

"Am I supposed to trust the word of the enemy?"

"*Enemy* is a rather discordant term."

"Then what would you call people on opposite sides of a war?"

He thought a moment. "Spectators in a game of chess, awaiting a just outcome."

"Spectators? Well, *spectators* can walk away from a game. And this *spectator* is going to do just that. Good day, sir." She stood.

"You can't go until you've had tea. It wouldn't be proper. Please take your seat."

She sat back down.

Private Coats entered and set a second china teacup and saucer on the desk next to the pot of tea. "Shall I pour, sir?"

"Yes, thank you."

The soldier poured from the white china teapot into a matching cup on a saucer and then held up a small crystal pitcher. "Cream?"

The girl's eyes widened, and she shook her head.

From the expression on her face and from her comment about the firing squad, Charles suspected she thought they might be trying to poison her. He gave a nod to the private, who poured cream into Charles's cup.

Charles motioned to the soldier to put half a teaspoon of sugar in his cup.

Coats gave him a questioning look but spooned in the sugar. He then held up the bowl toward the girl. "Sugar?"

She eyed the bowl and nodded.

The soldier ladled in a spoonful. When the girl still eyed the sugar, he scooped another spoonful. She nodded, evidently liking her tea sweet.

Charles excused the soldier and held out the girl's cup of tea to her.

When she hesitated, he said, "You saw him pour everything from the same containers. It's safe."

She took her cup and stirred it.

He sliced open a scone and made a production of stirring the clotted cream and the strawberry preserves before spreading some of each on both halves. He handed her a plate with one portion of the cut biscuit. He'd made sure she could see that he was eating and drinking the same as he gave her. So, unless he was poisoning himself, she would know the food and tea were safe.

She tilted her chin up. "Is this to be my last meal?"

Her tone wasn't that of fear, but more like a challenge.

"You seem to think we English are barbaric. I assure you, we are quite civilized." He took a bite of scone and a sip of tea. "When I am confident you are sufficiently refreshed, I will see you safely out of camp and on your way home."

"You expect me to trust the word of the en—"

"You wound me. Please refrain from calling me that, for I would never think of you as my enemy. You are far too fair."

"Then how should I think of you? A spectator armed with a sword and gun?"

He glanced at the weaponry he always wore. "Think of us both as residents on opposite sides of a fence. We are just trying to determine to whom this fence belongs."

"Well, *this fence* is definitely American." She nibbled the scone.

Was she baiting him? "The Oregon Treaty states otherwise."

"I am afraid you need to brush up on your reading. The treaty clearly portioned these islands to America. Anyone can see they are south of the forty-ninth parallel." She sipped her tea.

"Yet they are on the English side of the strait."

"The wrong strait. Haro is the strait in the treaty, not Rosario."

"I beg to differ. It is all in the interpretation."

"And the English are obviously masters at misinterpretation."

This girl was fun to parry with.

"We would argue otherwise."

"Argue all you like. That still wouldn't make you right."

They could go round and round on this and never acquiesce. He sat on the corner of his desk. "Do tell me your name."

"It is inconsequential. After today, you'll not have need of it."

"Pray tell why not?" She was a cunning one.

"You will either release me or have me shot."

He laughed. She was certainly amusing. "Did you enjoy our formal garden?" He'd watched her on a number of occasions gazing at the garden from her perch on the hill. She'd even ventured down a few times when she'd evidently thought no one was around, but never advanced inside the gate. He had always let her be. But today he'd been helpless when she and her brother entered. He had been inexplicably drawn to her.

"It is very beautiful. I grudgingly admit it is one thing the English can do."

He smiled. "So we are not all deplorable?"

"Just because one can grow a flower or two does not make one inherently virtuous."

"We do know how to brew a fine cup of tea." She couldn't possibly argue with that.

She seemed to think a moment as she took a sip. "It's all right. I've made better."

She was not going to give him anything. Except the formal garden. Sort of. "Did you like the scone?"

"It was a little dry."

A laugh burst out of him, overtaking him before he could contain it.

This girl was a spark of charming diversion in an otherwise languid "war." He wished he'd made her acquaintance on her first visit to the formal garden. Life here the past two months would have been far less tedious.

Her mouth twitched.

He couldn't tell whether she wanted to laugh as well or break down in tears. He would like to see her laugh. Or at least smile.

He was sure she had the most lovely of smiles.

Chapter 2

Rachel schooled herself. She would not laugh. She would not laugh. She would not laugh.

It had been fun to banter with this officer. He so wanted her to find good in the English. The English ways had long intrigued her. And he was so easily baited.

Though she loved listening to his accent, could listen to it all day, she needed to get home. "I am quite refreshed and will take my leave now, Leftenant."

He stood and bowed to her. "I will escort you." He ushered her outside.

She headed straight for the hill.

"Do you wish to visit the gardens before you depart?"

"I wish to get to the hill. The garden is the straightest route."

"You can't scurry up that hill!"

She had scurried down that hill and back up. Many times.

"Let me get a buggy and drive you home," he said.

She couldn't let him do that. Papa would shoot him on sight. Then this war would really heat up. "I will be fine. Good day." She pushed through the garden gate and hurried across to the one on the other side.

He laughed. "You aren't seriously going that way?"

"Yes, I am."

"I can't let you climb a hill."

"I assure you, I will be fine." The sooner she was away the better. She'd already lingered far too long. She started up the hill.

"I promised no harm would come to you whilst you were in my charge, and I intend to keep that promise." He climbed behind her.

The faster she got to the top, the sooner he would be on his way.

Halfway up, he said, "Your dress is all dirty back… here."

He was looking at her backside? Not that he had much choice from where he was. She stopped to tell him she would manage without him, but straightening caused her balance to shift, and she felt herself tilting backward. She flung her arms out to steady herself, but to no avail.

Her descent stopped abruptly.

"I've got you." His hands were about her waist. "You're safe."

Was she?

He set her upright. "Aren't you glad I'm escorting you now? You could have tumbled all the way down."

No. If it weren't for him, her concentration wouldn't have been broken and she never would have lost her balance. "Thank you."

At the top, she thanked him again so he could leave.

He glanced around. "Which way is your home?"

She waved her hand toward the south.

"But there isn't any path. How will you find your way?"

She pointed. "Through those bushes, keep the water to the right, and I'll be home in a jiff." It would take her close to an hour, tromping around bushes and over fallen trees. "I can find my own way."

"Now, what kind of gentleman would I be if I let you off on your own?"

"English."

He took in a slow breath. "I am a gentleman first. And a gentleman worth his salt wouldn't allow a lady to walk home unattended. I shall protect you from harm."

"Harm from what?"

"From wild animals, of course. Mountain lions, bears and wolves."

She forced herself not to laugh at that ridiculous notion. "There isn't anything more dangerous than little ol' foxes in this forest, and they wouldn't get close enough to people to harm them. The only animals I need worry about are the two-legged kind."

He cracked a smile. "Then I shall protect you from them."

It was quite unlikely there would be any other people in the forest between English Camp and the American residences. He fell into step beside her but soon had to fall back for her to squeeze between bushes.

He stopped and gripped his sword hilt. "I heard something."

"Maybe it is one of your bears or mountain lions." She kept walking.

He caught up with her. "Are you truly not afraid of bears and mountain lions?"

"If I were to meet face-to-face with either, I would be terrified and in need of assistance. But since there are neither on these islands, I am not afraid."

"No bears or mountain lions? Fascinating."

"Didn't you know that?"

"I only arrived two months ago and haven't learned about the wildlife."

She came to a downed tree. Traversing it would be most unladylike. But going around on either end would be impossible at this juncture.

The leftenant bent on one knee with his other raised. He patted his level thigh. "Step here."

How gallant. She did and climbed over.

As the leftenant was about to hoist himself over, he spun around, drawing his sword with a swoosh.

At the sharp end of his blade stood Lindley brandishing a stick. "Leave my sister be."

Rachel leaned on the log, trying to reach for the leftenant's arm to stop him. "Don't hurt him. He's my brother." She'd thought Lindley had run home.

The leftenant lowered his sword, and Lindley struck. The leftenant caught the stick, twisted and disarmed Lindley. He sheathed his sword. "If you are going to come at a man with a *weapon*, you need to know how to wield it."

The foolish leftenant handed the stick back to Lindley. As he reached for another stick from the ground, Lindley swung at him.

"Lindy, no!"

The leftenant's hand flew up and grabbed the stick, but he didn't look up. He disarmed Lindley again. His stick was longer than her brother's. He broke it over his knee to the same length and handed Lindley back his.

Lindley swung.

The leftenant blocked. "Spread your feet apart like this and bend at the knees. It helps you move and avoid your opponent's blows."

Lindley did as instructed and swung.

"Good. Hold farther down on your sword."

Rachel rolled her eyes. It wasn't a sword. It was a silly

stick. This was better than a second slice of pie to her brother. She would never get him home now.

Charles parried with the boy for a couple of minutes before he noticed the girl tramping away through the forest. "Your sister has gone off."

Lindley shrugged. "She don't like sword fighting. She says boys are silly. Well, I say girls are silly."

"We should catch up to her."

The boy scrambled over the log, and Charles followed suit. His uniform would be in dire need of cleaning when he returned.

Charles watched the girl up ahead lithely maneuvering through the underbrush of berry bushes, weedy grasses, some kind of wild rose and skunk cabbage. "What is your sister's name?"

"Rachel. Didn't you know that?"

"She refused to tell me."

The boy shook his head. "See, what'd I tell you? Girls are just plain silly."

If she could hear their conversation, she gave no indication of it.

"How old is she?" Maybe in a couple years, if this peaceful war was still *raging*, he could come calling.

"Twenty."

Charles jerked his head around and stared at the boy. He must have misunderstood. "This sister. Rachel."

"Rachel is twenty. Alice is eleven. Winnie is seven. Edith is five. And Priscilla is just a baby. I'm twelve." The boy advanced on a bush and gave it a slashing blow.

"Hold your sword up. If you are attacked by something a bit more vicious than a bush, you want to be able to ward off your opponent's blows."

Lindley assailed a maple sapling next. His stance was improving—not by much, but improving.

"If she's twenty, then she must have a husband," Charles said. Why this husband would let her traipse through the forest alone was confounding.

"Ew! No!"

"A beau?"

The boy shook his head.

That pleased Charles. Though he didn't know why.

Even with the lad pausing to assault the undergrowth, they gained on the girl.

After more than a mile of walking up and down the terrain, over branches, around bushes and trees, Rachel stopped and turned. "You can return to your camp."

"My honor would be blemished if I did not see you safely home."

"For *your* safety, it's best if you don't go any farther. I have my brother to see me the rest of the way. And with his *sword* lesson, I'm sure I will be quite safe."

She was teasing him for instructing the boy.

He scooped up her hand.

She drew in a sharp breath and held it.

Did she think he was going to bite her? He bowed over her delicate fingers. "Milady, my day has been brightened by your presence. You have utterly charmed me. 'Good night, good night! Parting is such sweet sorrow…'"

"'That I shall say good night till it be morrow.'"

Was she simply finishing the quotation? Or was she promising to return? He hoped the latter.

He gazed into the oceans of her eyes. Twenty? Why wasn't this beauty married? Certainly she had suitors. If she had not been American and on the opposite side of this nonexistent war, he would have been on her doorstep, asking to call on her.

Lindley made a false retching sound, wrapped his arms around his middle and stumbled away.

So dramatic interludes must be commonplace in this family.

"My knight has run off. I should go and see to *his* safety."

Charles dipped his head. "Good day, milady."

Rachel's heart thudded in her chest. The leftenant had been so gallant. And it had been lovely and fun until Lindley tried to come to her rescue.

"Where have the two of you been?"

Rachel jerked her head up.

And there was Papa's disapproving look she'd tried to avoid this morning.

"We lost track of time."

"You have worried your mama."

She knew better than to point out that Genevieve was not her mother. Instead, she nodded. "I'm sorry, Papa." She hoped Lindley didn't tell Papa where they had been.

Lindley gripped her hand behind her back and squeezed. "Sorry, Papa." He would not tell.

"If those English didn't live within shouting distance, I wouldn't worry so much. You must be more careful."

They were a bit farther than shouting distance, but not much. "We will," she said.

Her brother echoed the promise.

Papa shook his head, unable to keep up his stern face. "Your mama saved you both some supper. Go eat."

"Thank you." She kissed Papa on the cheek and then scurried into the house behind Lindley. She wasn't as hungry as her brother must be. She'd had the benefit of tea and half a scone with clotted cream and delicious strawberry preserves. And the scone had been so delicate it almost melted on her tongue. Her mouth watered just thinking about it.

Genevieve looked at Lindley and then at Rachel, put

her hand on her chest and gave a sigh of relief. "Sit. I'll bring your plates."

"We can get our plates." Rachel saw them warming on the stove. "Sorry for making you worry. We lost track of time." She handed Lindley his plate, and the two of them sat.

After she had eaten, she set about washing the supper dishes.

Papa's and Genevieve's voices drifted in through the open window. Papa said, "I don't know what I'm going to do with her."

Rachel felt it was safe to assume Papa was talking about her. He always thought he had to *do* something about her. She didn't need fixing. Wasn't she fine the way she was?

"Don't be too hard on her," Genevieve said.

"She should be married by now, or at least considering marriage. She seems perfectly content to traipse around these woods like a wild animal."

"She's not acting like a wild animal. The girl is a dreamer."

Rachel sighed at that. She did enjoy dreaming. Places she went in her mind were always perfect.

Genevieve continued, "There are no other young people her age on this portion of the island. There isn't much for a young lady to do. I think she goes out there and dreams of a knight on a white horse coming to rescue her."

And he was quite handsome.

"And you think that is better than running wild?"

"Of course not. I have tried telling her, life and love are not like she reads in books."

"If I take her books away, maybe that will straighten her out."

"She would only hate you."

She could never actually hate Papa, but she would be quite angry at him.

"Then I will find her a husband."

Rachel dropped a plate in the washtub, splashing dirty water on herself.

Genevieve gasped. "You would arrange a marriage for her?"

"Why not? Daisy and I had an arranged marriage. That turned out fine until she got sick. And *our* marriage was arranged. Are we doing so badly?"

"It would break her spirit. You are forgetting two very important things. We knew each other before the marriage was arranged. Same with Daisy. And you, my husband, are a very easy man to fall in love with."

"Then what am I to do?"

Rachel could picture Papa hanging his head, shaking it.

"Suitors. Find a few young men willing to come calling and let her choose."

Rachel held her breath for Papa's reply.

Silence dragged.

Lord, please let Papa give me a choice.

"Very well. I'll speak to a few men after church tomorrow."

Rachel let out her captive breath. *Thank you, Lord, for Genevieve.* Suitors at least gave her a say in the matter. But she knew that no suitor Papa brought 'round would be wearing an English uniform.

Or have golden flecks in his eyes.

Chapter 3

The next morning, Charles stood at attention in a clean, pressed uniform in front of his commanding officer.

Captain George Bazalgette leaned back in his chair. "I hear you held an American girl captive yesterday."

"She wasn't a captive, sir."

"Then you did hold her here."

"I wasn't really holding her. It was only high tea, sir."

"But you kept her against her will."

Charles didn't believe it was against her will, not really. She could have run off after her brother at any time. But he supposed the nuance of the interlude wouldn't translate to his commanding officer. "It was all perfectly harmless, sir."

"Harmless?" Captain Bazalgette stood abruptly, his chair scraping against the floor. He braced his hands on the smooth, polished desk and leaned forward, his face red. "If she tells a solitary soul, or even hints to one person, that she was here and might have been detained, this ten-year peace could blow up in our faces. So far, we have had only a Berkshire boar as a casualty in this war. Both sides would like to keep it that way."

"But we have amiable relations with the Americans."

"It has taken a great deal of work to keep things peaceful. There are those on both sides who would like to see this little armistice break into a full-scale war. Not only could we lose possession of these islands, but also there would be both American and English bloodshed. I will not have one of my officers responsible. I will see you out of Her Majesty's Navy and back home, *dishonored*, before I will allow that to happen. Am I clear, Lieutenant?"

Discharged from the navy? Scandalous! He would be disgraced in his family as well as society. Unable to hold his head up. And for what? A bit of a lark with a pretty young girl? "Yes, sir."

"If I get wind of your doing anything like this again, you will be reprimanded and on the first ship back to England. You won't even be able to get a station shining seamen's shoes."

Charles swallowed. "Yes, sir."

"Dismissed."

Charles saluted, then put the toe of his right shoe behind the heel of his left, did a sharp about-face and marched out.

As he strode across the grounds, he caught sight of his brother Brantley, just a year older, talking to Melissa. He headed in their direction but stopped when close enough to hear the couple's conversation.

His brother's wife's face was twisted in fury. "How could you have allowed us to be stationed in this place? There is no society. No real parties. No theater. By the time we get back to England, I will be a nobody. Completely forgotten."

Charles veered away, not wanting to get caught in the

middle of that discussion again. He headed for the formal garden.

His brother had his standing in society, but at what cost? His wife was a horror to live with. She spent all his money and denied him access to her sleeping chambers if he so much as spoke crossly to her. His other two brothers hadn't fared any better with their society matches.

He would rather remain single than live like that. Then a certain raven-haired beauty came to mind. Rachel would charm any man she met. Not out of manipulation and deceit as many women did, but out of her purity of heart, quick wit and intelligence. Men were not used to women with such qualities. Or at least women who revealed them.

Nay, Rachel was a rare gem in the midst of counterfeit jewels.

A gem out of his reach.

Rachel sat in the window seat, watching rivulets run down the glass. For days it had poured. Usually she didn't mind so much being cooped up in the house because the children were at school for most of the day.

But she longed to be walking in the forest. She loved being out there. When this rain let up, she would walk and walk. She closed her eyes and pictured herself amongst the massive trees, hiking, not stopping for anything. Just moving.

She could almost smell the freshness of the forest, the sodden earth, the crisp air. She imagined reaching out with her hand to a sword fern, the rain droplets on her palm.

In her mind, she walked farther and found herself standing on the hill overlooking English Camp. Then she was down below in the garden. The *lef*tenant stood before her. His hazel-brown eyes with the gold flecks studied her. He smiled and brushed her cheek with his fingers. She leaned into his touch.

Priscilla fussed, and Rachel jerked open her eyes. Sadly, she was at home and not in the forest. Genevieve had lain down with the baby, giving Rachel this respite.

She opened her book and pulled out the flattened purple flower. It had stained the page of her beloved book, but she didn't care. She sniffed the limp bloom. Still sweet.

Soon Papa's wagon came up the road with the children. Her repose was over. She stood and slid a risen loaf of bread into the oven.

Papa was all smiles. Usually this much rain put him in a sour mood. She loved it when Papa came home in good spirits.

He kissed her on the cheek. "Where is your mama?"

"She's lying down with Priscilla."

"It's good of you to let her rest. Did you have a pleasant day?"

She nodded. She had gotten to read.

"Good. I have a surprise for you."

Her smile matched Papa's in width. "You do? What is it?"

"Patience. You will see later."

Giddy with anticipation, she set about finishing the supper preparations.

When a knock sounded on the door, Papa's grin grew wider. "Rachel, dear, would you get that?"

Since when did Papa want her to answer the door? But she went, and Papa followed right behind. "Your surprise."

On the porch stood an exceedingly handsome gent in common clothes. Tall with broad shoulders, brown hair. Eyes the color of a favorite hen she had raised from a chick years ago. And his smile could make most any woman swoon.

Papa stepped forward and shook the man's hand. "I'm glad you could make it."

"Thank you for inviting me to supper."

"This is my daughter Rachel. Rachel, this is Mr. Anderson."

Mr. Anderson doffed his hat and shook the water off it. "Call me Buck."

If this was the man whom Papa thought would make a good suitor for her, honoring him wouldn't be difficult. And gentlemen callers wouldn't be so hard to take, after all.

Buck made polite conversation with Papa throughout supper. Rachel had to force herself not to stare.

Lindley made his fake-in-love face at her from where he sat across the table next to their guest.

She swung her foot under the table to kick him and get him to stop.

Lindley twitched.

Buck jerked his head around to look at her.

Oh dear. Had she kicked him instead? Or had Lindley bumped him? She stabbed a bite of fried potato and popped it into her mouth.

Buck turned back to Papa's question.

After supper, Papa and Genevieve left her and Buck in the parlor, the pocket doors open a wee bit. Buck seemed to like to talk. She didn't mind. It gave her a good reason to stare at him. But then he said something that drew her attention away from his handsome features and to what he was saying. "What was that?"

"I expect a wife of mine to work alongside me in my orchard."

There had been more. She was sure of it.

"She should take in laundry, keep the house clean, have supper ready for me, keep the children in order. I want to have a lot of children. When they get older, they will be a big help in the orchard. I plan to expand."

Yes, there had been more. A whole lot more. "Your wife will be a busy woman."

"Idle hands are the work of the devil."

She squinted. Was his nose crooked? "Your children will hardly have time to work in the orchard while in school."

"Well, the boys can go for a year or two to learn their numbers, but they will be in the orchard during picking time."

A year or two? "And your daughters? Will they receive a full education?"

"Girls, go to school? What do they need with reading and writing and numbers just to keep house? The Good Lord never intended for girls to go to school."

"So your daughters will be illiterate, and your sons will have only a rudimentary ability to read?"

"Such things aren't necessary in running an orchard. Why waste the time?"

"Reading is not a waste of time."

"Reading is for the weak of body. 'If any would not work, neither should he eat.' The weak-minded, as well. Teaches people not to think for themselves."

She didn't believe that the Lord wanted His people to be ignorant. And she could use a verse out of context just as easily. "'But I would not have you to be ignorant, brethren.'"

"Yes, that is for the men, hence it says 'brethren.'"

She wanted to throttle him. He could twist anything in his favor. She had a mind and will of her own. She was by no means lazy, but he would not like having her as a wife. Could she convince Papa?

Buck had moved from the topic of education back to his orchard. "My trees grow very well. I sell all I grow and for a good profit. Those foolish English will pay any price I name for a sweet, crisp apple."

She turned slowly to him. "You sell your apples to the English?"

"Peaches, cherries and pears, too. But I charge them thrice what I do Americans. Those soldiers are so daft."

When finally he left, complaining about wasting so much time away from his orchard during this critical period just before harvest, Rachel breathed easier.

But Papa beamed. "He was a polite, nice fellow."

Lindley made a retching sound.

Papa turned on him. "You stay out of this." He faced her, waiting for her assessment of Buck Anderson.

She could tell him that Buck wanted a wife only to be slave labor and to bear children who would be more labor, and that they should all be ignorant. Papa might respond that she shouldn't be too choosy, and it wouldn't be so bad because Buck could provide well for her. But she knew just what tidbit Papa would be most interested in. "He's sympathetic to the English."

Papa's smile melted. "What? I can't believe that."

Rachel nodded. "He sells his fruit to them." She would leave off the part about him charging them so much more, because Papa might view that as a good thing.

"I don't care how nice and polite he is. I forbid you ever to see him again."

She sighed dramatically. "If you say so, Papa."

Papa walked off, muttering. "I can't believe I welcomed him into my home."

Rachel smiled to herself.

"Good riddance." Lindley saluted toward the door. "I like the *lef*tenant better."

Rachel gripped her brother's arm and marched him to his small bedroom. "You hush up about that. If Papa finds out, you'll get a whipping, and I'll never be allowed to leave this house until I'm forced into an arranged marriage." She pointed her finger in his face. "And if I have to marry someone I don't want to, I will make your life miserable. I promise."

"Papa wasn't around. I'm not a dunce."

"Don't slip up," she threatened him as she left.

She went to the room she shared with three of her half sisters. Sitting on her bed, she pulled out *Romeo and Juliet* and let it fall open to the page with the pressed purple flower.

Chapter 4

Rachel laid the burlap sack she'd brought on a log at the overlook to English Camp. She'd slipped away while Genevieve was nursing Priscilla. Sitting on the sack, she looked out over the camp. The garden still held some of its summer colors, but was fading as fall progressed with autumn flowers. The English sure knew how to plan a garden to make the most of vibrant blooms from early spring through fall.

She let her gaze travel to the lawn the soldiers marched on. Several men milled around, looking small down there. She stared harder, but not one of them appeared to be Leftenant Young. She knew now that he had a particular gait to his stride, a tempo to his walk. She'd noticed him before that day they met last week but hadn't known his name. Now she had a name and a face to go with the uniform. And laughing hazel-brown eyes. She could tell when he was teasing by their twinkle.

It was just as well she didn't see him. She shouldn't

be here. And she definitely shouldn't be pining over an English officer. Nothing could come of it. She forced her gaze back to the garden crowned with russet and gold chrysanthemums as well as other flowers in a glorious autumn bouquet.

Her attention was jerked back to the lawn, or rather the main structure on the lawn. The one that the leftenant had taken her inside. An officer had exited the building and turned to speak to someone still within. When he turned back, her breath caught. It could be him. The way he carried himself was just like the leftenant.

He strode up to a young woman in a fancy azure gown. The two spoke. The woman waved her closed fan and shook it at the leftenant. He appeared to be pleading with her. She stiffened and shook her head. The leftenant's shoulders slumped.

And Rachel knew that her leftenant had a sweetheart or wife. It had been fun to pretend for a week. But her childish musing had come to an abrupt end.

"Looking for someone?" a male voice asked behind her.

Rachel jumped up and spun around. Leftenant Young stood before her. *Her* leftenant. She looked back to the officer on the field. The woman turned and walked away from him.

Leftenant Young came up beside her. "Ah, my brother and his *delightful* wife."

That was why the man had walked like her leftenant. Not really *her* leftenant…but the one she'd met.

He adjusted his pose like an actor on a stage. "I will pretend 'twas I you were seeking." Like Romeo with Juliet.

She turned back to the leftenant. She couldn't admit that.

"Be still. Speak not." His eyes twinkled. "For if you say, nay, 'twas not I you sought, my heart will be crushed."

He was teasing her again. But at least he didn't expect a serious answer. "Far be it from me to crush something so fragile as a soldier's heart." She doubted his heart was at all fragile. "I would never be so cruel, so I will keep mine answer to mineself."

He smiled broadly and bowed to her. "Milady, I'm ever so pleased you have returned. I was hoping to see you again."

"You were?" Her heart fluttered.

"Most certainly."

"I believe I—I mean, my brother and I caused you so much trouble the last time that I thought you would have been glad never to lay eyes on me again."

"The last time? So you haven't snuck here when I was unaware?"

One little word revealed so much. "The last time that I saw you."

His mouth twitched. "I see. A lady never reveals her secrets."

"Would you expect her to?"

"Nay." He bowed.

She sensed he was conceding some sort of win to her, but she wasn't sure exactly what.

He straightened. "I am so very glad you have come."

"Were you waiting up here for me?"

"I must confess I was."

That surprised her.

Then he looked down a bit sheepishly. "For the better part of a week and against rational judgment."

He'd waited for her? Hoping she would return? A thrill rippled through her. "Against rational judgment?"

"Military officers have their secrets, as well."

She should have expected as much. "Were you hoping I would return so that you could make me walk the plank?"

He chuckled. "Walking the plank is something pirates

make their prisoners do." He hesitated for only a moment before clarifying. "On a ship. Out at sea."

She knew that. But it was fun to tease him back. He had a nice smile.

His hazel eyes twinkled. "The best I have to offer the lady is the pier."

"Not the same. Perhaps throw me in your jail, then?"

"We don't call it a jail. It's a brig. And I believe it is already occupied at the moment."

"Then why hope for my return, if not to punish me for trespassing?"

He reached inside his coat and retrieved a flat parcel wrapped in thin brown leather and tied with a strip of thicker leather.

From the size and shape, her first thought was that it was a book. She reached for it but then, thinking better, pulled her hand back.

"Go ahead. Take it. It's for you."

"I'm sorry, sir. I cannot." But she wanted to.

"Why not?"

"It wouldn't be proper for a lady to accept a gift from a man she hardly knows." Especially an English officer. Papa would skewer her and then force her to marry the first man he could find. Even if he was old or terrible. Or both.

The leftenant wiggled the gift. "Just open it."

Why tempt herself? "I appreciate your kind gesture, sir, but I cannot accept your gift."

"Then at least open it so I can see if you like it."

She stretched out her hands toward the package and then closed them. Papa would never know that she simply unwrapped it. Her fingers uncurled. But she would know. She fisted her hands. "Truly, I wish I could." She shook her head but didn't take her eyes off the gift.

"Then allow me to unwrap it for you."

Excitement coursed through her. She would get to see what it was, after all. And if Papa chanced to ask her if she'd ever accepted a gift from the leftenant, or from any man, she could honestly say no.

The leftenant pulled at the leather bow. Ever so slowly. She wanted to grab the leather end and yank the strip off. So she tightened her fists instead to make her hands obey.

He stopped just short of freeing the one loop of the bow. "Mayhap you're right. Mayhap this shouldn't be opened."

She jerked her gaze to his face. Not open it?

"You probably aren't interested in what's inside anyway."

He was teasing her again. And she'd fallen for his trickery. "As a lady, I would be remiss to not at least see what is inside to acknowledge your kindness."

He held out the gift. "Would you like to finish?"

Yes! she wanted to yell. Instead she said, "You go ahead. I wouldn't want to deprive you."

He reached for the strip and then stopped. "I'll unwrap it if you admit you have the minutest curiosity as to the contents."

He was sly. Dangle the bait, pull it back when he knew his prey wanted it more than anything, and make her beg. "I can guess what it contains."

"Do tell?"

"It is obvious. A book."

"Yes. Obvious. But what book?"

As to that she didn't have a clue. And she was desperate to know. "Perhaps one of Shakespeare's other plays."

"Which one would be your guess?"

Macbeth? Othello? The Tempest? "A Midsummer Night's Dream."

He chuckled. "That is a fun play. But this is not a Shakespearean play. Or any other play."

She had a limited knowledge of authors. "A collection of his poems, perhaps?"

"Close."

She huffed a breath. But he wasn't going to tell her. And she doubted she would ever guess it. "Very well. I do have the minutest bit of interest in what you have brought. Only because you have enticed me."

With her confession, he quickly finished opening the parcel. He held out the book, which lay on the leather covering in his outstretched hands. The red leather volume had wear marks from much reading. It was a book of poems by someone named Sir Walter Scott. She wasn't familiar with him but was eager to peruse his writings.

"Even though he is a Scotsman, I like his work." The leftenant leaned in and whispered conspiratorially, "Don't tell Mother England."

"Pray tell, why not? Isn't Scotland part of England? The whole British Isles?"

"Scotland as well as Ireland are like children throwing a tantrum, struggling to be independent. But in reality, they are better off under England's protection."

"Independent? Like the United States of America? We fought and won."

"Ah. The colonies that got away."

"And we will win these islands, as well. They belong to us."

"That is not a matter for us to decide. Let's not sully the moment with politics. We have digressed." He pushed the volume toward her.

She dared not touch it lest she never want to put it down. After all, it was a book. One she'd never read before. How could she resist? She had only a handful and had read them each several times. When she'd been in school, she'd had access to a variety of others. But since completing school, she didn't. Papa brought home one now and then for her. But this was a book she'd never heard of before.

"Go ahead. Open it. I know you want to."

She stared at it.

"Certainly it wouldn't be improper to just look at it?"

Of course not. But she knew herself. She wouldn't want to give it up.

"Let me." He tossed the leather covering aside, turned the book to face himself and flipped it open.

Her heart sped up in anticipation of the words it contained. And at the man standing in front of her, offering her words she'd never read before.

"Here. I think you'll like this one.

"'O listen, listen, ladies gay!
No haughty feat of arms I tell;
Soft is the note and sad the lay
That mourns the lovely Rosabelle.'"

She closed her eyes and listened to his accent measuring out the verse in slow rolling time. The highs and lows, and where he chose to add emphasis, told her how he felt about the piece. His cadence. As though the piece had a life pulse.

But she'd best pay attention before the poem ended.

"'There are twenty of Roslin's barons bold
Lie buried within that proud chapelle;
Each one the holy vault doth hold—
But the sea holds lovely Rosabelle.

"'And each Saint Clair was buried there
With candle, with book, and with knell;
But the sea-caves rung and the wild winds sung
The dirge of lovely Rosabelle.'"

He paused and took a deep breath before breaking the spell with ordinary words. "Did you like it?"

She opened her eyes. "It was quite lovely."

"Tell me. What is it about?"

She wasn't sure, and she sensed he knew that. She had paid more attention to his languid tones and accent, to the flow of verse, and not so much to individual words and their meaning. "Rosabelle was a ship that sank."

"Anything else?"

What could she say? That she wasn't really listening to the poem but to his voice? "Any good poem needs to be studied to be fully appreciated."

"How true." He handed her the volume.

She took it before she thought better and let the weight of it sink into her hands.

"You pick one," he said.

Since she already held the book, what could it hurt now? She flipped through the pages and found a short one titled "Lucy Ashton's Song."

"'Look not thou—'"

"Shh." The leftenant put his finger to his lips and looked past her. "Quickly. Someone's coming."

She hadn't heard anything but hastened quietly. She was practiced at moving through the forest with very little sound.

He tucked her behind a broad tree trunk and stood, facing her.

She focused on steadying her breathing to keep it quiet and stared at the ornate brass buttons on the leftenant's chest. His whole uniform was pressed and neat. And he smelled of some earthy spices.

First came the voices and then the crunching of the forest floor underfoot. Two men who weren't worried about being quiet. Good thing for her. They were probably English soldiers. She wondered why the leftenant felt the need to hide. Perhaps he simply didn't want to explain what he was doing on the hillside in the middle of the day.

The men's voices and footfalls drew closer, and she held her breath. They spoke of their wariness of this war. "Either give these bloody islands to the Americans or take them by force. 'Tis a fool's mission to just sit here and rot like a compost heap."

If those men knew one of their officers could hear them, they wouldn't speak so freely. They apparently had passed as close to the tree as they were going to, because their voices diminished into the distance.

She remained silent until she hadn't heard the two men for quite some time. She looked up at the leftenant.

He was gazing down at her as though studying her. Not at all upset about the soldiers' comments.

Her heart palpitated at his nearness and the intensity of his golden-flecked eyes.

Charles regarded this young woman standing before him. Her sea-blue eyes studied him boldly. She was rare indeed. "Why do you come to English Camp?"

She seemed startled by his question. As though she hadn't really expected him to speak. Or perhaps hadn't expected the question. "I like looking at the garden."

The garden? "Once you had seen it, there would have been no need to see it again. And the first time you didn't even know it was there."

"Actually, I did know. There was talk that the English were so foolish to have a fancy flower garden, and no wonder they lost the Revolutionary War."

Was she goading him? He let it pass. "You made it clear when I walked you home that your father doesn't approve. Do you disobey him regularly?"

"I didn't actually disobey him. He never directly forbade me to come."

Charles raised his eyebrows. "But you knew if you asked his permission, he would forbid you." The flicker of her gaze away told him he was right. "You're a passive rebel." Much like himself. His parents hadn't directly ordered him to find a suitable socialite wife, but it was implied in every undertone of every communiqué. He had subtly avoided the topic. Part of the appeal of serving so far from home.

"I wouldn't say a rebel. More a naturally curious person."

"Once your *curiosity* was satisfied, why return?"

"My curiosity is rarely satisfied. There is much of interest in the forest. On the whole island."

"If he directly forbade you to come, would you stay away?"

She hesitated and then nodded. "I would have to."

"So you are careful in coming."

She closed the book. "I should be going." She handed it to him.

"Please keep it."

She stared at the book as though she wanted to. "I cannot. If my father found it…"

She needn't say more. He clasped the book. He didn't want to risk her not being able to return. He walked her back over to the log with her burlap sack. Quite fortunate that the soldiers hadn't seen it. After folding the coarse fabric, he handed it to her. Then he bound up the book in the leather, tying it securely. "I will leave the book hidden under the front edge of this log." He leaned over the log and tucked the book there. "Next time you come, you will have it to read."

"Thank you!" She smiled at him.

And he felt as though he'd just been knighted by the queen herself.

"I must go."

He didn't want her to, but if he hoped to see her again, he must. "Shall I walk you?"

"Thank you, but no. I'll travel faster alone. I have already been gone longer than I should."

He, too, had been gone an unacceptable amount of time. He bowed. "Until we meet again. 'Good night, good night! Parting is such sweet sorrow…'"

She curtsied. "'That I shall say good night till it be morrow.'"

He was tempted to keep her there but knew he mustn't. She walked backward a few steps, then turned and hurried through the underbrush. Her ebony hair tied at the nape of her neck swished across her back. He imagined it felt as silky as it looked. He watched her until she disappeared quickly in the thick undergrowth.

He hastened to the path above the officers' quarters. No one would think it strange if he emerged from that direction, but they might question if he scuttled down the hill he'd escorted an American girl up the week before. He slipped between two cabin-houses and came out onto the narrow carriage road. He, of course, didn't live in one of these homes. They were for the married officers. Being the lowest ranking officer and unmarried, he had a small room within the barracks.

"Where have you been?"

Charles spun around to face his brother. "I was patrolling the perimeter."

Brantley looked displeased. "Captain Bazalgette has been searching for you."

This couldn't be good. "I'll go right away."

"Don't bother. I told him that I sent you on an errand. I heard about your indiscretion last week."

It wasn't an indiscretion. Everyone was making more of it than it was.

His brother gripped his shoulder. "You have to watch

what you do. You can't have any kind of blemish. Not only is your military career at stake but also your social standing. We may be thousands of miles away from London, but word gets back."

Charles didn't believe anything that happened here on these remote, inconsequential islands would have any effect on his social standing. His parents certainly wouldn't fault him. Would they?

Should he resist the urge to climb the hill in hopes of catching a few stolen moments with Rachel? The thought of never seeing her or teasing her didn't sit right with him. He would just have to be as careful as Rachel was being.

Chapter 5

At the knock on the door, Papa encouraged Rachel to open it. She knew that suitor number two stood on the other side. She took a deep breath to steel herself before swinging the door open.

Another handsome man, his hair a chestnut brown. He bowed deeply to her and spoke in a heavy Irish brogue. "Carrig O'Leary at your service, milady."

Rachel blinked, not believing this man stood on her porch.

Papa nudged her. "Invite him in."

Rachel stepped back. "Please, come in." Papa was allowing this man into his home? When Carrig went to greet Genevieve, Rachel leaned closer to Papa. "Papa? This man is from the British Isles. I never thought you'd let an Englishman in our house."

"Not an Englishman. An *Irish*man." Papa's eyes brightened. "The Irish dislike the English as much as we do. As they say, 'My enemy's enemy...'"

"'…is my friend,'" she finished.

Papa patted her back. "Exactly. I think you are going to like this one."

She was sure she wouldn't. But she smiled and toddled off like an obedient daughter. She might have to work harder to find something that Papa would find adverse about him.

But Carrig said all the right things, complimented Genevieve's cooking and gave attention to Rachel's half sisters and brother, even the little ones. By the end of supper, Rachel was even beginning to like him. Well, except for his strong dislike of the English, which he made sure he mentioned several times. To Papa's great delight.

"The English are brutes who think they have the right to rule over the world. People came to this country to escape their tyranny."

Papa beamed at that comment.

Soon, Rachel was left alone with Carrig in the parlor. He motioned toward the settee. "Please have a seat."

She would have preferred to sit in the chair, but he stood in front of that. It would be rude for her to move around him and sit there. So she nodded and sat in the middle of the settee, leaving no room for anyone but her littlest sisters to join her on either side. She hoped he would back up into the chair. But he didn't. He wedged himself between her and the arm of the furniture. She scooted to the end of the settee before he completely sat down. Could she move to the chair without being rude?

He gripped her hand, effectively keeping her in place. At least for now.

Her insides twisted. She didn't like him so much anymore. He hadn't shown his aggressive side with Papa around. She pulled her hand free and smoothed her hair. "What do you do?"

"I work at a cobbler shop. You'll never be without shoes with me for a husband."

"Husband?"

He was a bit bold and getting ahead of himself.

"I've heard the talk. Your da is looking for a husband for you. He favors me. I could tell."

Fortunately for her, Papa didn't have the last word. He was allowing her to have a say.

"You're a very pretty girl."

"Thank you." But she was a young woman, not a girl.

When he reached for her hand again, she turned and stood in one fluid motion, then crossed to the fireplace.

Edith ran into the room.

Rachel scooped her up. "What are you doing?"

"Read me a story." Her five-year-old sister held up a book of nursery rhymes.

Rachel looked out the open door. Lindley stood at the table in her view with a smile. She mouthed, "Thank you."

Carrig came over. "Why don't you run along, little girl? Your sister can read you a story later."

Rachel took the book. "Sure, I'll read you one."

It was a game. Rachel read one rhyme. When it was done, her sister would beg for another and another. Edith had learned this from Winnie, who had learned it from Alice. Rachel sat on the settee so she and Edith were in the middle of the seat, not leaving enough room on either side for Carrig.

Carrig eyed the settee, conceded defeat and sat on the edge of the chair opposite them.

Rachel struggled not to smile. She read the first rhyme, "Mary, Mary, Quite Contrary."

When the rhyme was finished, seven-year-old Winnie ran in. "Read *me* one."

She settled Winnie on the other side of her, looked up at Carrig and shrugged.

After seven rhymes, Carrig stood. "I should go. I'll come another time. When things aren't so busy."

She hoped not. She stood, as well. "It was nice of you to visit."

He took her hand in his warm, moist one. "Until the next time."

She forced a gracious smile. She would have to talk Papa out of a *next time*.

Once Carrig was gone, Papa looked at her expectantly. "I liked him."

"I know, Papa."

Papa's grin flattened. "You didn't like him?"

"He was a bit forward in the parlor."

"Well, you're a pretty young lady. Any young man might forget his manners momentarily."

She would concede that even she had lapses in manners. "Papa, is his being Irish a good enough reason to make him your son-in-law?"

"There was more to him than his heritage. He was pleasant. I'm not a young lady, but he is a fine-looking fellow."

"Yes, he is. But I just can't see myself married to him. Please, Papa."

Finally, Papa agreed he wouldn't invite him back. But he promised to find someone better.

Someone better? She pictured the leftenant and smiled inwardly. But Papa would *never* invite him into his home.

The next gentleman suitor was several years older than Rachel. At least thirty. And once again, Papa had brought home a striking man. Malcolm Williams, a sheep farmer.

Once they were alone in the parlor, he studied her as though she were a horse—or perhaps a sheep—under consideration for purchasing. He sized her up from her head to her feet and everything in between. He even circled around her. Did men really think that any lady liked to be treated this way? If he attempted to open her mouth to examine her teeth, she would bite him.

When she moved to sit in the chair, he put a firm hold on her elbow and maneuvered her to the settee.

"You aren't exactly what I had in mind for a wife, but you are young and could likely bear me heirs."

Now that was romantic. Just the way to win a lady's heart. He wasn't exactly what she had in mind either. "And what are you looking for?" Then she would do everything she could *not* to resemble his ideal in any way.

"I had hoped for a wife more pleasant looking, but you aren't all unpleasing on the eyes."

That stung, but not really. She would need to care about this man before anything he said hurt her. Carrig had said she was quite pretty. A sheep farmer? And Malcolm thought she was beneath him? He must have a lofty view of himself. It wasn't as though there was an excess of young ladies this far west. A lady could be choosy, but men didn't have that luxury. If a man found a wife who was even plain, he counted himself fortunate. And Malcolm didn't have a wealth of money to attract several women to choose from. Why were all men so difficult?

Well, not all men. There was a certain English leftenant who had been both charming and most pleasant on the eyes.

In that moment of her distraction, Malcolm leaned into her, attempting to steal a kiss. His supper-infused, hot breath fanned her face.

She pulled away. "What are you doing?"

He remained close. "You don't expect me to offer marriage and a home if I don't like even kissing you?"

"I don't expect you to press your advantage." She moved to get up.

But he put his hand on the arm of the settee on the other

side of her, trapping her. "I am not going to have wasted my evening here and not at least leave with a kiss."

"I don't have a mind to let you kiss me." She pushed on his arm.

"I like your spunk." He leaned closer to take that kiss.

"Let me go!"

When he was about to succeed, the parlor doors slid open with a bang. Papa and Lindley stood in the doorway. Genevieve stood behind them, holding baby Priscilla.

"Get out of my house!" Papa growled.

Malcolm stood. "You are going to have a hard time finding a husband for that one." He tromped out.

Genevieve sat beside her. "Are you all right?"

Rachel took a calming breath. "I'm fine."

"Are you sure?"

"He was just trying to steal a kiss." But her hands still shook slightly, so she clasped them together in her lap. At least she didn't have to worry about Papa ever inviting Malcolm back.

Claiming distress from her suitor the night before, Rachel had little trouble convincing Genevieve to let her go walking in the woods.

"Are you sure you want to go out there alone? Wouldn't you feel safer in the house?"

It had been in the house that she hadn't been safe. Not that Papa had been very far away. The moment she had been about to call out to him, he had come to her rescue. "I have never had any trouble with the woodland animals. I feel calmer out in the forest."

"Very well. But don't be too long. I worry, you know."

She appreciated Genevieve's concern, but she would feel much more at ease being able to get away.

Soon she stood on the hill overlooking English Camp. Scanning the area, she didn't see the leftenant either up on the hill or down below. She leaned over the log to see if the book was still there. Pulling it out, she noticed it was bulkier than she remembered. Turning, she sat on the log.

In her rush, she had forgotten to bring the burlap sack to sit on, but the log wasn't too wet. Her skirt would get damp, but she could easily tell Genevieve she'd sat down to rest. And that was exactly what she was doing. She untied the leather strip and folded away the leather covering.

But instead of the book cover, she saw a wax-coated muslin cloth. She folded that back, as well. And there sat the poems. The leftenant must have come back to wrap the volume in the wax cloth to protect it further from the moisture. He was quite thoughtful. And she liked that he thought to protect a book. Not everyone would do that.

Opening to the first poem, she read it through. A rustling sound caught her attention, and she turned. A chipmunk sat on the end of the log with some sort of seed in his paws. He considered her a moment before he scolded her, twitched his whiskers and scampered off.

She flipped through the pages until she found the "Rosabelle" poem and read it over and over. The leftenant was right. She did like this one. It had a mysterious, haunted quality that made her want to unlock its secrets.

Charles sat at his brother and sister-in-law's supper table.

Melissa dabbed at her mouth between bites. "Dear brother-in-law, I fear I have fallen down on my duties as your sister. So I have taken measures to correct that." She stabbed a coin of cooked carrot and daintily plucked it off her fork into her mouth.

"And what duties would those be?" He couldn't even imagine. He glanced to his brother, who shrugged and gave him an "I'm sorry" look.

Sorry for what? Charles's stomach clenched. "What have you done?"

She smiled coyly and dabbed at her mouth with her napkin again. "I have written to two of my cousins and a good friend, telling them all about you. Truly, they already know much. London society eagerly awaits the return of a handsome, eligible bachelor."

He'd thought he was safe being away from his mother. But evidently not. "What did you tell them?"

"That you would make a fine husband and are looking for a suitable wife."

"I'm not looking for a wife. You may tell them so."

"Well, not here, obviously. The caliber of ladies on these remote, backwoods islands is both limited and below your station." She shifted to face him better. "You don't even know who the young ladies are that I have chosen. I have put a great deal of thought into their selection. Any one of them will make you a wonderful officer's wife. Each is quite pretty and comes from a family with excellent social standing."

He was sure they did and were as boring as a stick of furniture. A moan escaped. He cringed. Bad manners.

"Oh, don't make it sound like a death sentence."

It might as well be. Why couldn't people be content with him being a bachelor? No doubt his mother would have a titled lady or two she hoped he'd entertain the idea of marrying.

His three older brothers were sufficiently married to ladies who came from families with *excellent social standing.* He hoped that had made his parents content to not pressure him. But in case they became tempted, he'd volunteered for this tour of duty as far removed from London society as he could get, hoping *society* would forget about him.

Bachelorhood suited him.

But he did picture one young lady at his side. A lady who wouldn't be wounded at the slightest provocation, real or imaginary, a romantic with a flare for drama. A lady who was intelligent and could keep up with him in a conversation, who could keep him on his toes and guessing. A lady who was interesting.

For the first time, bachelorhood didn't seem so permanent.

Or agreeable.

Chapter 6

Rachel pictured the leftenant's teasing hazel eyes as he'd tempted her with the book of poems. She had enjoyed reading them the other day and couldn't wait to go back to read more. And ideally he would be—

Alice nudged her. "Is that right?" Her eleven-year-old half sister sat on the settee next to her, holding up her yellow-and-blue quilt block.

Rachel adjusted her focus to the fabric. Alice's seams were getting straighter. Once the block was pressed flat and quilted in the full piece, the waviness of the seams wouldn't show. "That's fine. You're getting better." On her other side, Edith sagged against her, sleeping.

Alice smiled. "What's next?"

Rachel showed her the next two pieces to be stitched together.

Lindley tromped into the room a bit too noisily.

Genevieve looked up from the chair where she was nursing Priscilla. "Lindley, what are you doing?"

Lindley had his bow and arrows in hand, and his coat and boots on. "I'm going hunting."

What was Lindley up to?

"No, you are not," Genevieve said.

"I'm going to bring back supper."

"I already have a sausage stew started on the stove."

"Then I'll bring back supper for tomorrow. Boys at school were saying that they've seen a lot of rabbits."

Why was her brother being so insistent?

"Your father is not here to go with you," Genevieve said.

"I've gone hunting by myself before."

He was up to something. Rachel could tell by the way he twisted his left foot.

"Not with my approval."

He pointed his bow tip at Rachel. "Then make her go with me."

"I don't want to go hunting." It was terrible to watch a cute, furry bunny hopping along one moment and dead limp the next. Rachel didn't have trouble eating them. She just didn't like to see what she was eating alive first. Yet she had no problem with the squawky chickens. Silliness.

Genevieve nodded. "There, your sister doesn't want to go."

Lindley turned his soulful brown eyes on Rachel. "Pleeeease." Then he winked.

Rachel quickly looked at Alice, but she'd had her head down, working, and missed the wink. Rachel was curious about what her brother was up to. "All right. But I'm not carrying rabbits, and I'm not skinning them."

He nodded. "I'll even give you the pelts to line a hand muff."

That would be nice. Soft and warm. As Rachel stood, she adjusted Edith, laying her down on the settee.

Genevieve looked up at her compassionately. "You don't have to go."

"You know how restless he gets with only us women for company. I wouldn't mind the walk." And she wanted to know what her brother was scheming. Had he winked just to pique her curiosity enough so she would go with him? Or was he truly up to something? She put on her boots and coat and grabbed the Jane Austen novel she was rereading.

Lindley waited for her outside. As soon as she stepped out the door, he was off.

"Lindy, wait." But he didn't.

She hurried after him. "What's the rush? You're going to scare all the rabbits."

It was apparent he wasn't really out to hunt. He finally slowed.

She caught up with him. "All right. What are you up to?"

"Hunting," he said innocently.

"And what exactly are you hunting that you haven't already scared off?"

"My quarry's not in this part of the forest." He took off again, bounding through the woods.

She shook her head. With all the noise he was making and the disturbed forest floor and bent underbrush, she wasn't going to hurry. He would be easy to follow. Soon it dawned on her where he was headed. English Camp. But what could be his quarry there? He wasn't thinking to start a war all on his own, was he? She quickened her pace.

When she caught up to him, he was looking out over the camp. She grabbed his arm and spoke sternly. "You aren't going to shoot any soldiers. I thought you liked Leftenant Young."

"Not shoot them. Watch them. I do like the leftenant. Why do they say *lef*tenant instead of *lieu*tenant?"

A voice came from behind them. "Because it's the proper pronunciation." The leftenant stepped out from behind a tree. "You Americans have mucked up the queen's English."

Rachel's breath caught at the sight of him, and her heart danced. His slight smile told her that he was glad to see her, as well. "Just because we Americans are independent and choose not to pronounce things in an archaic way, doesn't mean we are mucking things up."

He stepped closer. "This coming from a lady who fancies old Shakespearean plays in an *archaic* style of speech."

He made a good point. And she liked the way he pronounced things. Everything. "They are poetic. And serve a different purpose than everyday conversation."

"Touché." He bowed with a flourish, moving one arm in a circle.

Lindley stepped between them, facing the leftenant, and thrust a stick at him. "Show me more sword fighting."

"Lindy, *Leftenant* Young doesn't want to."

"I would love to spar with you. But you must call me Charles."

Lindley nodded.

The leftenant turned to Rachel and dipped his head slightly. "You, too, milady."

"And if I refuse?"

He snatched her book before she realized what he was up to. "I will keep your book until you agree." He looked at it. "*Emma.* Jane Austen. I haven't read this one. To be completely honest, I've only read the beginning of one. I can't even remember the title. She's too flowery for my taste." He waggled the book. "Call me Charles, and you can have it back."

She wanted to use his first name. It was more intimate. But at the same time, she wanted to tease him. She sat on the log and reached down for the book of poems without looking. All she could come up with was a handful of dead, damp leaves.

"Looking for this?" He was smirking and holding up the poems in his other hand.

Lindley jabbed the leftenant with his stick. "Come on. Let's sword fight."

With both books in one hand, Charles took the second stick that Lindley offered him and raised it to block her brother's blow. He waved the books toward Rachel, taunting her, while still warding off Lindley's strikes. He didn't seem to need to pay much attention to defend himself against a twelve-year-old boy.

She would just have to be content to watch their tomfoolery. But she quickly bored of that and walked over to the leftenant, holding out her hand.

"What do you say?" he asked.

She curtsied and spoke in a highbrow accent. "May I please have my book...*Charles?*"

He chuckled and handed her both volumes.

Lindley jabbed him with his stick. "Got you."

With a last smile to her, Charles turned and got busy about the business of swordplay. With a swish of his "sword," he quickly disarmed Lindley and then gave her brother instructions on how to improve.

She opened *Emma* and began to read. She glanced up and watched Charles maneuvering with ease. Charles looked her way and winked. Focusing back on her book, she tried to block out Lindley's grunting and the talking. Concentrating on the story proved to be impossible. She could still pretend to read. She wished Lindley hadn't come. But if not for Lindley, she wouldn't have been able to come today. And she would rather be a spectator than not see Charles at all.

Maybe Lindley would get bored and leave. But she

knew he wouldn't. Not having any brothers, Lindley liked the male attention.

Rachel liked the leftenant's attention, too.

Charles quickly tired of the swordplay. He wanted to sit with Rachel and read poetry or quote Shakespeare or tease her. He looped his stick in a circle and once again disarmed his opponent. "I think that's enough for one session."

Lindley sat on the ground. The boy was more tired than he'd let on. "Have you ever killed anyone?"

It seemed boys of any culture were fascinated with death and killing. Charles understood the fascination. He'd asked the same of his father and oldest brother. It was a mental preparedness for what could lie in one's future. To know how to handle it if faced with bringing about the death of another. To know whether you would be strong enough to handle it if you had to. "I am pleased to say that I have not."

"Would you?"

"I guess I wouldn't have joined the military if I didn't think so." Actually, he still didn't know. Being an officer was the family business. He hadn't really had any other choice. "If I were fighting for a worthy cause. To protect the weak and innocent. To defend my homeland. Yes."

"Would you kill an American for the San Juan Islands?"

No one had died in this war so far. He hoped it stayed that way but knew the tide could turn and catch them all in a bloody battle no one wanted. "I hope it doesn't come to that."

"But if it does?"

He had never seriously thought that was a possibility. But it hung in the air like leaden clouds before it rained. "I honestly don't want to kill anyone."

Rachel stood next to her brother. "He wants to know if you'll kill our papa."

Charles shook his head. "No. Of course not." But he didn't even know her father or what he looked like, so he wouldn't know whether he was shooting at him if this war turned violent.

"He will fight alongside the American soldiers." Rachel stared at him with sad eyes. Eyes daring him to lie to her and tell her he wouldn't shoot her father if standing face-to-face with him in battle. "You would have no choice."

The look of desolation in her expression broke him. He sensed she had contemplated her father's death before. By him?

"We need to go." She walked away.

Lindley dropped his stick and followed her.

Charles stared after them. He was indeed playing with fire. Not only could his actions with Rachel ignite this peaceful war, but also he could be faced with the very real possibility of killing her father. The father of the only lady he'd ever seriously cared about.

He had true affection for her. He didn't know whether that was because she was forbidden to him, or because she had spirit and was delightful. Enjoyable to tease. A pleasure to be around. Comely. Charming. Fetching. Captivating. Enchanting. Lovely.

He sighed.

He sensed if he faced her father, he wouldn't be able to kill him. Charles would fall on the battlefield first.

He cared more for Rachel than he had realized or intended. He would rather die than hurt her. But he must stop any further foolish thoughts of her. She was American, after all. His commanding officer would be livid if he knew Charles was up here with her. Not to mention his parents. They would be shocked at his consorting with an American. She would never stand up to their ideal of a proper lady. Maybe that was why he was so attracted to her. She was different. Fresh. Endearing. Alluring. Winsome. Everything the ladies back in England were not.

He was such a fool. Nothing could come of his time spent with Rachel. Nothing but futile longing.

Rachel's hands shook. She moved through the forest as quickly as possible. She hadn't thought about it, but she knew Papa would fight again. She had been terrified ten years ago when the war first started, and Papa had taken up arms to defend the islands. The fact that the war could start again ripped her to the bones. The thought of Papa and Charles facing each other on the battlefield shook her. She didn't want either of them to kill anyone. Especially not each other.

"Rachel, do you think he'll kill Papa?"

She stopped and faced her brother. "No!" She didn't want to think about that. She couldn't.

"But—"

"I said no. Everything is peaceful. No one is going to shoot anyone else. Do you hear me?"

Lindley nodded. "I don't want them to kill each other either."

She struck out again.

If she walked fast enough, she could outrun that horrible thought and her own fear, couldn't she? The picture of Papa aiming his musket at Charles and Charles aiming his gun back wouldn't go away. She tried to shake it before either fired. The war was peaceful. No one had died. She prayed it stayed that way.

She had grown quite fond of the leftenant. She liked him a lot. She wasn't sure how or why it had happened. But she knew she mustn't see him ever again. If Papa found out, he would start the war to protect her honor.

Then it would be her fault if either of them died. Yes, the answer was to stay away.

She hurried into the house.

Genevieve asked, "Where are the rabbits?"

Rachel said, "He scared them all away. I'm not feeling well. I'm going to my room."

"You look a bit pale." Genevieve put her hand on Rachel's forehead. "You don't have a fever. But go rest."

Rachel was glad that Genevieve didn't fuss over her and let her go. She crawled into bed still dressed, trying to ward off the frightening images.

Her dreams reflected her troubling thoughts. Papa faced Charles. Each held a gun on the other. She screamed, "No!" as they both fired. She ran between them. But it was too late. It was all her fault. She startled awake with tears on her cheeks.

Edith lay snuggled next to her. She pulled her little sister closer and held on to her.

She would never go back to English Camp. She couldn't.

Chapter 7

Rachel took a deep breath before opening the door to the next suitor. She was determined to find good in this one. Someone to make her forget about Leftenant Charles Young. Her Romeo. Her forbidden love.

On the porch stood a good-looking man with black hair and blue eyes similar to her own. Though handsome, he wasn't as good-looking as the first three suitors. But maybe that was for the best. Maybe he wouldn't be so supercilious.

He bowed with a flourish. "Milady, I am so very pleased to meet you. Hugh Dawson, at your service."

Except for the lack of an English accent and the name, Charles could have said those very words to her.

He stepped inside. "I would have brought the young lady and the missus of the house flowers, but alas, there were none to be found."

"That's quite all right," Genevieve said. "Supper is almost ready."

Rachel stared at Hugh with dreamy eyes, trying to conjure up affection for him. But she couldn't.

Everyone scuttled to sit, Papa said grace, and dishes were passed around the table.

"Tell me, Hugh, what do you do?" Papa asked.

"I've done a great many things. I was an actor for a while."

Papa wouldn't like that. Though he paused in his chewing, he didn't say anything.

"I have done a little farming, both vegetables and dairy. I've picked fruit, worked with hogs, mended fences, gone on a cattle drive, been a reporter, done some mining, worked in a mercantile, been a sailor on a ship, harvested crabs and climbed a mountain." Hugh punctuated his list by taking a bite of stew.

He had certainly done a great many things in so short a life. Papa should like that. Hugh could do anything.

"Why so many jobs?" Papa asked in a way that told her he was suspicious of something.

"Haven't quite found what suits me. And it allows me to travel around. See the world. I don't like to stay put in one place very long. But I have finally found my calling."

Papa raised a curious eyebrow. "And what is that?"

"I've started my first play. I'm going to be a playwright."

He didn't just say that. Though *she* liked the idea, Papa would not.

"A playwright?" Papa stared at Hugh.

"That is a person who writes plays."

Papa's words were measured. "I know what one is."

Hugh should not have assumed Papa to be uneducated or simple-minded.

"How do you expect to support a family *writing plays*?"

The final two words seemed to taste bitter in Papa's mouth.

Rachel wanted to tell Papa that there were some very successful playwrights but knew he would not take that observation well.

"I suppose I will have to find a strong wife who doesn't mind working. But she would have to be willing to travel around from town to town, across the country and around the world."

Rachel would love to travel abroad.

"Around the world?" Papa asked. "What about a house?"

"We won't have a house. We'll sleep under the heavens as God intended."

"What about when children start coming? You'll settle down then and have a house?"

"I don't see a need to. Maybe we'll get a wagon to travel in. Like gypsies."

Papa clenched his jaw. "I will not have my daughter live like a gypsy, never knowing if she'll have food in her stomach."

Though traveling sounded nice, gypsy life did not.

"Certainly not your fair Rachel." Hugh waved toward her with a flourish. "She's not cut out for that kind of life."

"Then why are you here?"

"Free food. I can usually find kind and generous people such as yourselves. I rarely go long without a good meal." He turned to Genevieve, who was stifling a laugh. "Your stew and biscuits are delicious."

"Rachel made them."

Hugh turned to Rachel. "You will make some man a good wife."

But not this man. He wasn't looking for a wife, and Papa wouldn't allow this man to be his son-in-law. Both she and Papa were relieved. Hugh had absolutely no ambition. At least he'd made the meal entertaining.

After Papa realized Hugh was not marriage material,

he stopped peppering their guest with questions. So Rachel took up the slack in the conversation.

"What kind of plays do you write?"

He held up a single finger. "Just one play. It's rather tragic. It's the story of a young man without a home who doesn't know where his next meal will be found."

That sounded a little autobiographical.

"The man spends the length of the play searching for the father he never knew. He is always one town behind his father."

She wondered if Hugh was looking for his own father. "Does he ever find him?"

"In the final scene, the man finally is in the same town as his father. Someone tells him that his father is over at the bank. He goes there, and the bank is being robbed. The robber shoots him in the stomach. The robber is his father. And he says, 'Pa, why?' and dies in his father's arms. The father doesn't know what the man is asking about—why he shot him, or why he left him as a small boy? The father is caught and hung."

"That's not a very happy ending."

"Life ain't always happy."

"Sounds like you will be another Shakespeare with tragic endings to your plays."

"Nah, it'll be nothing like those Shakespeare plays. Mine you will be able to understand."

He couldn't see any parallels? It didn't matter. "So is your play finished?"

"Not yet. But I'm close."

"How much do you have written down?"

"None of it." He tapped his forehead with his index finger. "I have it all up here."

She could think of nothing more to say to him.

After Hugh left, Papa shook his head, then shook it again, and then shook it some more.

Genevieve touched his shoulder. "What's wrong?"

"Amos." Papa chuckled. "He's having a good laugh about now."

"How so?"

"He told me this fellow was perfect for Rachel. Said I had to invite him over. Rachel would like him. I should have known he was setting me up."

Rachel spoke up. "I wouldn't say perfect, but I did like him." But not for a suitor. Hugh had been interesting.

Papa turned serious. "No, I'll not be inviting him back. He's not right for you. I would be derelict in my duties as your father if I agreed to you marrying someone who couldn't support you."

"And I would be derelict in my duties as your daughter to entertain another thought of such a man." She kissed him on the cheek and heard Papa sigh as she walked away.

The next two suitors weren't any better. Papa was growing wary. She hoped he would give up this quest and let her grow into an old maid. That would be better than marrying a man she didn't love. Or loving a man she could never be with.

After being detained three separate times, Charles was finally able to go up the hill undetected. Or at least he hoped he was undetected. He went to Rachel's spot. He looked around but didn't see her. He closed his eyes but couldn't hear anyone in the vicinity. He leaned over the log that hid the book. The parcel hadn't been touched in two weeks. He knew because he'd carefully placed a leaf and a twig on top of it so he would know if it had been moved. They were both right where he'd put them a week and a half ago.

He hadn't liked how the conversation had ended the last time he and Rachel had seen each other. Talk of war and killing.

When he first arrived on the island, he'd been frustrated with having little to do that was meaningful. It had seemed to be a waste of military might. An agreed-upon stalemate. Now he saw the wisdom in keeping the peace. No need to shed blood unnecessarily. Once the shooting started, it would be hard to stop. Retaliations would run rampant. Neither side would like the other. Any friendly relations built between England and the United States of America since the Revolutionary War would be destroyed.

And now he had a personal stake in praying the peace continued.

Indefinitely.

If the time came, he would have to follow orders, but hoped he wasn't sent to the same battle as any of Rachel's relatives or friends. He would never be able to face her.

"What are you doing, little brother?"

Charles spun around to face Brantley. "Trying to collect my thoughts."

"About what?"

Too many things. "What we are really doing on these islands."

"We are keeping the peace."

"Are we? Or just postponing the inevitable?"

Brantley spoke in measured words. "We are keeping the peace."

"You don't wonder if one side or the other or both will get tired of this stalemate and change everything?"

"No. The American officers want the peace as much as we do. It is best for both sides."

"The officers, yes. Even the enlisted men. But there are other factors to consider."

"Like what?"

"The civilian population. How did this whole fiasco start? An American farmer shot a British pig over potatoes. The officers might have agreed to this peace and be bound by orders, but the general population isn't. What if there is another pig/potato incident? Or something that really matters?"

Brantley narrowed his eyes. "Is this about that girl?"

It might have started out that way, and she might be *his* strongest motivation behind keeping the peace, but he had finally seen the delicate balance of this whole situation for the first time. "It's been ten years. Shouldn't this be settled by now? Isn't this a waste of time and resources?"

"No. The San Juan Islands are the gateway up the straits to the British holdings there. If we have the islands, we control the straits. These islands are an advantageous military position."

Brantley was right. But how would possession finally be determined, if not by war?

"You need to forget about that girl."

He doubted he could ever do that. Try as he might to dispel her image from his mind, she consumed his thoughts and settled in his heart.

Chapter 8

Their vegetable garden had reached its end and everything had been harvested just in time for the cold snap that brought the first frost. With that frost, their three apple trees needed to be picked. So for the past three weeks, Rachel and Genevieve had done little else other than can fruits and vegetables for the winter. And Rachel did little else other than think about Leftenant Young while working. The pattering of the soft rain on the windowpane lured Rachel's thoughts through the forest. She missed going to English Camp and seeing him. She struggled to remember the words of the poetry, listening for his accented voice reading them.

"Are you all right?"

Papa's words jerked her back to the present. "What?"

"You have been standing there, staring out the window, unmoving, for fifteen minutes with that towel in your hands."

She looked down at the cloth twisted into a tight ball. She set it aside.

"Now, Rachel," Papa said in that coddling voice he sometimes used with her when he wanted to convince her of something, "you know that it is what is on the inside of a man that counts."

"Yes, Papa."

When someone knocked at the door, she opened it to Henry Olson and almost gasped but stopped herself in time. His face had the misfortune of getting in the way of a freckle attack. Freckles were on top of freckles, bleeding into one another, all vying for space. It would be easier to count the spots of pale skin than count the freckles. And then there was his hair. Though trimmed short, it was as orange as carrots. Maybe that was why he kept it short, so it wouldn't be blinding.

He spoke very softly when he spoke at all.

Once everyone sat down at the table and the blessing was said, the food was passed around and plates were filled.

No one spoke for a minute or two until Papa said, "Henry, tell my daughter what you do."

Henry put down his fork, dabbed at his mouth with his napkin, replaced the napkin on his lap and lifted his gaze to hers. His voice was so low she had to strain to hear him. "I work at the bank." He picked up his fork and resumed eating.

Papa smiled. "A good job. He owns his own home, as well."

Henry once again set down his fork and dabbed his mouth before speaking. "Technically, the bank owns it until I pay off the mortgage."

Supper was slow and relatively quiet. Sitting in the parlor after supper wasn't much better. Henry seemed like a sweet fellow. She could find no fault with him. She would try extra hard to like this one. Allow Papa to invite him back.

That thought caused a hollow place to open up inside her, and she thought about Charles. Even though she knew she shouldn't, her daydreams always drifted back to him. The harder she tried to forget him, the more she thought about him. Why? He was only a friend.

Though Henry hadn't been there long, he stood. "I've had a lovely time."

"You're leaving?"

He nodded.

And with that he left.

She was a little disappointed. If he'd stayed longer, maybe she could have started caring for him and forgetting about Charles. But she doubted Henry could ever make her forget.

Papa came up to her and draped his arm around her shoulders. "He was a nice man. And he can provide well."

"He was nice. But I'm not sure."

"Don't let all those freckles taint your opinion. Get to know him. Give him a chance."

"I will, Papa." She lifted her shawl off a peg and wrapped it around herself.

"Where are you going?"

"Out to the barn to see if I can find where Mariposa hid her kittens."

"All right." He kissed her forehead. "I just want what's best for you."

"I know." Taking a lantern, she opened the door and stepped out into the cool, damp night air.

In the barn, Mariposa, a tricolor calico, wound between her legs. Rachel looked where she'd last seen Mariposa and her five kittens. They should be opening their eyes. But they weren't there.

"Mariposa, where did you hide your kittens?" She set the lantern down and picked up the mama cat.

Mariposa started purring right away.

Then Rachel thought she heard something and listened. A faint mew. "Where are they, Mariposa?"

Rachel heard the mew again. The loft. "Mariposa, say it isn't so. You didn't carry your kittens up there?"

The cat, hearing her babies, jumped from Rachel's arms.

Rachel watched the cat climb onto a crate, jump to a barrel and then onto a narrow ledge and leap across open space, landing easily on the edge of the loft.

Rachel grabbed the lantern, hurried up the ladder and heard the hay rustling in the far corner along with a mew. She headed over and found Mariposa nursing her kittens. She didn't have the heart to take one of the kittens while it was feeding. So she sat down beside the mama and petted her. Mariposa leaned into Rachel's hand and purred. "This is a good place. Winnie and Edith won't be able to bother them up here. But is it safe once your babies start moving around?"

Rachel leaned her head back against the wall and closed her own eyes. Immediately, the image of Charles's face came to mind. She successfully forced it away. Then the memory of his accent floated through her mind. She tried to banish it. "'Farewell: thou canst not teach me to forget.'" Her love of *Romeo and Juliet* proved to be a hindrance.

She must concentrate on something else. Henry perhaps? No, she had thought enough about him for one evening. So she opened her eyes and focused on the cat. Her soft fur and gentle purring.

Another noise.

She shifted her gaze and listened hard. She heard it again. And then at the bottom of the ladder. "Papa?"

A head popped up above the floorboards. "Just me. May I come up?"

Charles! She jumped to her feet and trotted over. "Yes. What are you doing here?"

He finished the climb and stood in regular clothes. No signs of being an English officer. Only his accent betrayed his heritage. "You haven't come to the camp in a while."

It had been a month. Long. Lonely. Tedious. "I thought it best."

"Best? Why?"

"I have no desire to start a war."

"Neither do I. I just wanted to make sure you were all right."

Even though she shouldn't be, she was so very glad he'd come. "Do you want to see some kittens?" She didn't even wait for him to answer but led him over to the corner. She maneuvered through the hay to the other side of Mariposa and sat.

Charles sat where she'd been before. "What's her name?"

"Mariposa."

"Like the lily."

"Yes." She was surprised he knew that.

"How many kittens?"

"Five. You want to hold one?" She scooped up a black-and-white kitten who'd finished eating and was sleeping and plopped it into his hands.

"This fellow is cute. I like his white chin and whiskers."

The kitten also had a white upper chest and white paws. He started mewing.

Mariposa disturbed her other four kittens from eating, which caused them to start mewing, and carefully took the kitten from Charles and put it back with the others.

Rachel looked at Charles, not knowing what to say. Though she was glad to see him, she couldn't tell him so. He shouldn't even be here. But she didn't want him to go away. She had missed him. So she said nothing.

Charles also said nothing.

She thought the silence would be awkward, but some-

how it wasn't. At least at first. Then it became very awkward. She should say something. "I'm sorry."

"For what? You have done nothing to be sorry for."

"I'm sorry I went to English Camp. If I hadn't gone,
none of this would have happened."

"You mean you're sorry you met me."

"No—I mean…" She conceded defeat to herself. "It
would have been better if we hadn't met."

"Nothing has happened. No one knows. Is it so wrong
to be friends?"

"Friends? Is that what we are?"

"Of course. What else would we be? And don't say
enemies."

She wasn't going to. "Friends." This encounter was
strange. Not like their others with the teasing and the ban-
tering. She wanted to bring that back. The fact that he had
come here meant something different. Something more.

To return to their lighthearted banter and to test his
true knowledge of *Romeo and Juliet*, she said, "'O, then,
I see Queen Mab hath been with you.'"

He gave a soft laugh. "'She is the fairies' midwife, and
she comes / In shape no bigger than an agate-stone…'
Testing me?"

"A little."

"So you have all of *Romeo and Juliet* committed to
memory. And you like Jane Austen. Did you like Sir Walter Scott's poems?"

"The ones I have read."

"You haven't read them all yet?"

"Poems are like juicy strawberries at the height of
the season. They are meant to be savored. Eat them too
quickly and you are never satisfied. I read one poem, over
and over, each time I go."

He shifted in the hay. "Do you have a favorite so far?"

"That would be like choosing one food. A cherry is

as different from salmon as from bread or milk and yet they are all equally good in different ways. How would one choose?"

"I guess one couldn't." He picked up a piece of straw and rolled it between his fingers. "Name a poem you read that you liked."

She pretended to think a moment but knew her favorite. "'It Was an English Ladye Bright.'"

"I should have guessed."

Tilting her head, she asked, "Why?"

"It is much like *Romeo and Juliet.* That is a good one."

"Are there any bad ones?"

"There are a few I don't care for. What other books have you read and liked?"

She scratched Mariposa's neck. "I like the Brontë sisters."

His eyes twinkled. "I should have guessed."

"Why do you say that?"

"*Romeo and Juliet.* You had a Jane Austen book with you the last time. 'It Was an English Ladye Bright.' The Brontës make sense. You are a true romantic."

She was glad the lightheartedness was back.

"Would it be too forward of me to ask who that young man was tonight?"

She hadn't expected Charles to have seen or known about the suitors. "You saw him?" She felt her cheeks warm. "How long have you been here?"

"I confess, quite some time. Is he someone special?" Charles broke off the end of the piece of straw.

She supposed it was forward of her to answer, but she wanted him to know. Needed him to know. "No, not special. Papa is determined to find me a husband."

"So your father chose him. Is he nice?"

"I think so."

"You spent the evening with him, and you don't know?" He continued to break the straw.

"He was painfully shy."

"He doesn't sound like the manner of gentleman you would be content to marry."

"Well, he was nicer than the others."

"Others?"

Oh, yes, the others. Ones she had tried to forget. "Buck thinks that reading is a waste of time and that a wife is to bear children and work harder than he does."

"He is obviously not a true gentleman or he would know that a lady is to be adored and taken care of. You got rid of him, I hope."

"Yes, but I should warn you that he charges the English three times the price for his fruit than he charges Americans."

"Ah, Mr. Anderson." He picked up another piece of straw and pointed it toward her. "I've met him. And we know he charges us more. It's all for the sake of peace. Who else?"

"Malcolm didn't think I was pretty enough." She would leave out him trying to steal a kiss. His opinion of her looks was embarrassing enough.

"He's a liar, plain and simple," Charles said matter-of-factly. "Who else?"

"Hugh had no job, no home and no ambition."

"And he was no good."

"Bernard and…and…oh, I forgot his name."

"He obviously made a lasting impression."

She giggled.

"It's good you can laugh at all this."

It was good to laugh. "You shouldn't have come."

He tossed the piece of straw away. "I needed to see that you were all right. Please come back. If for nothing else, to read the rest of the book. Or I'll have to check on you again."

No. That was far too dangerous. "I don't want to risk starting a war."

"Technically, the war has already been started. We just haven't fought any battles yet."

She wanted to return but knew she shouldn't.

"You are always very careful when you come. Don't worry about a thing. No one is going to find out."

"Are you sure?"

"Who goes in that stretch of the forest but you?"

"You."

"Then you have nothing to worry about. I know you want to finish reading the book."

She twirled a piece of straw. "I'll think about it."

"Rachel?" Papa called from below.

She quickly put her finger to her lips.

Charles gave her a nod of understanding.

She stood and pointed to her spot. "Yes, Papa. I'm coming."

As she moved one way through the hay, Charles moved the other so it didn't sound like two separate people moving and he was more hidden in the hay. She grabbed the lantern and went to the head of the ladder.

Papa stood at the bottom. "Did that silly cat haul her kittens up there?"

"Afraid so." She turned and started down the ladder before Papa could decide to climb up. "I think I've annoyed her. She might move them again."

Papa took the lantern. "She'll likely leave them put. She knows Winnie and Edith can't get them up there."

She hooked her arm through Papa's. "Let's go inside. I'm getting a little cold." She hadn't noticed the nip in the air until then. She was relieved when Papa came with her without saying he needed to stay in the barn for anything.

She hoped Charles would wait a sufficient amount of time before trying to leave. Once in the house, she hurried up to her room and stared out the window.

Alice came in after a few minutes with Winnie and Edith and looked out the window, too. "What are you watching for?"

Rachel let the curtain drop back into place. "Nothing." She hadn't seen Charles leave yet, and she certainly didn't want to let Alice see and tell Papa that a strange man was leaving their barn. She would have to be content with her memory of their encounter.

After Charles visited her in the barn, Rachel was eager to go back to English Camp. She would be extra careful to not be seen.

When she arrived, she didn't expect to see the leftenant. He had duties. He couldn't just wander off whenever he felt like it. She sat on the log and reached for the book of poems. Something felt different, so she bent over more to get a look. There were two other leather-wrapped books. She pulled out all three and stacked them on her lap. She opened the one she was sure was the poems and then set it aside.

The next book was by Elizabeth Gaskell, a biography of Charlotte Brontë. The third book was called *Little Women* by Louisa May Alcott. She'd never heard of these books, but she had to admit her exposure to literature was quite limited on the islands.

"I thought you would like those."

She spun around at the male voice and saw Charles. Her heartbeat sped up, and her breath caught. "They look wonderful. I can't wait to read them."

"You should also try George Eliot. I couldn't get my hands on a copy, but as soon as I do, I'll bring it. I wish you could take them back to your house and enjoy them every day, not just when you come here."

"Knowing they are here for me to read makes me happy. Thank you so much. Where did you get them?"

"I borrowed them from my brother's wife." He sat on the log but not directly next to her. He left an appropriate distance between them.

"She must love to read, too."

"Nay. She thinks books make her look smart, especially when she can tell her friends she has purchased the latest in literature."

Rachel couldn't imagine having books that she never read. "Won't she miss them?"

"I doubt it."

"I'll be careful with them."

"I know you will. That's why I brought them. Every book should be read at least once."

She hoped to read them more than once. "You must think me a silly girl for traipsing through the forest to see a garden and for gushing over books."

"Never. Wait. Let me amend that. The first day I met you, I thought you were a girl. But I learned better."

Rachel was aware she looked younger than her years. "You expect me to believe you know my age?"

"I do. You are twenty, which makes you a lady, not a girl."

Rachel was shocked. He really did know her age. "How did you guess that?"

Charles tapped his temple with one finger. "I'm very perceptive."

She planted her hands on her hips. "I don't believe you."

He chuckled. "Lindley told me that first day."

"That's not fair. You know my age, but I haven't a clue about yours."

"Take a guess."

He couldn't be too very old.

"Go on, guess."

She squinted, studying him. She put her fist on her chin and tapped her lips with her index finger. She would guess early to mid-twenties. A perfect age. "Two score and a half a score."

He coughed in surprise. "Fifty? You wound me, milady."

"I'm sorry. Are you older?" She tried hard not to smile.

"You know I'm not. I'm half that minus one."

"Twenty-four."

"You're quick with numbers."

"Does a lady being able to do numbers surprise you?"

"I know a lot of people, both gentlemen and ladies alike, who would not have been able to figure that number so quickly in their heads."

"It wasn't a difficult equation."

"But still, you didn't hesitate or seem to have to think about it."

It really was nothing to be impressed over. She could solve more complex equations in her head. "So then, you think me a silly young lady."

"Never silly. You, milady, are an enigma."

"An enigma?"

"That means you are—"

"I know what *enigma* means." He must think her a simpleton.

He chuckled. "You lean more toward being mysterious rather than difficult to understand."

She liked being mysterious.

"But I also find you enchanting and delightfully fascinating."

She liked the sound of those words. A delightfully fascinating young lady who enchanted.

"On the outside, you may appear ordinary, but on the inside, you are extraordinary, full of wit and charm and intelligence."

But did he think she was pretty?

He tapped one of the books. "Read a poem aloud."

"Am I your servant?"

"I would never think of you in such a manner. I find pleasure in your accent."

"My accent? I don't have an accent. You, sir, are the one with an accent."

"And to me I have no accent. It is all in the ear of the listener."

She held the book out to him. "I read last time. It's your turn to flaunt your accent."

"Very well, milady." He took the volume and opened it, flipping through the pages until he stopped on a particularly long poem. "Prepare to be amazed at the *flaunting* of my accent."

She closed her eyes and listened to the smooth timbre of his voice, the way he pronounced each word, syllable and letter.

When he finished, she said, "That was beautiful."

He handed over the book. "Your turn."

"I need to get back."

"As should I."

Charles had been pleasantly surprised she'd come. He had been right suspecting she was avoiding him. But his visit to her seemed to have cured that.

He was glad he'd brought the books. They would give her reason to keep coming. With all of Melissa's books, Rachel would need to return for years to read them. But not if her father found her a husband.

That didn't sit well with Charles. He knew the pressure good-intentioned parents could place on their children to marry. He had always accepted marriage as a way of life for himself. Something to put off as long as possible, but in the end, inevitable. He would marry someone to please his parents even if he didn't love that person.

But for Rachel, he didn't like the idea one bit.

He watched her walk back through the woods until he couldn't see her any longer.

"So, she's the girl you are risking your career and social standing for."

Charles spun around to face his brother. "Brantley?"

"That was a sweet little interlude, but is she really worth losing everything?"

He did not want to have this discussion. He knew what his brother would say. He'd already given himself all the lectures. All the reasons he should stay away from her. But he'd failed in the execution of those intentions. So he changed the subject. "I'm sorry for the comment about Melissa and her books."

"No need to apologize. It's true. You should stay single as long as you can."

"Why do you think I volunteered for duty on this island? No one for Mother to match me up with."

"What about this girl?"

"She is just a friend." Truly, she could be nothing more.

"One does not risk everything for a young lady who is *just a friend*."

Chapter 9

Waiting until the English soldiers had gone inside for their afternoon tea, Rachel scurried down the hill and stood inside the fancy garden. She had hoped there would still be a flower or two left she couldn't see from above, but late November offered no blooms. The garden looked sad and lonely and cold. She shivered.

"Miss?" a voice said behind her.

She spun around to see two soldiers standing at the gate.

"You don't belong here. You'll have to come with us."

Could she outrun them and get up the hill before they captured her? She doubted it.

The soldier who had spoken for the pair motioned with his hand. "Come along. No one is going to hurt you."

She stared at him.

He entered the garden and came up to her but didn't touch her. "This way."

She mutely obeyed.

They took her inside the building she had been in before. One soldier waited with her outside an office that was not Charles's while the other knocked and then entered when commanded.

She could hear him speak.

"Sir, we have captured an American spy in camp."

Spy? She swallowed her urge to laugh. The thought that she was a spy was ridiculous, but this was a serious matter, being in English Camp uninvited.

"A spy? What need do the Americans have to spy on us? Bring him in." The voice sounded like Charles's but wasn't.

"Um, sir…"

"Just do it."

The order was snapped so sharply that the soldier outside with her straightened. She did, too.

The soldier came out and escorted her into the office. The officer behind the desk sat with his hands steepled and a stern look upon his face. But as soon as he saw her, his eyes widened, and he stood. "This is but a girl."

"Yes, sir. She was snooping around the formal garden."

The officer who looked and sounded a lot like Charles, who must be his brother, turned to her. "What is your name?"

"Rachel Thompson."

"Please have a seat, Miss Thompson."

She planted her feet. "I'll stand."

He came around the desk and studied her. He shifted his gaze from her to the soldier. "Bring my brother. Quickly and quietly."

"Sir, the men have all seen her."

"Go!"

The soldier scrambled away.

Rachel cleared her throat. "Would you just let me leave? There is no need for all this fuss."

"I agree with you. But, since you are already here, there is already a fuss." He pulled a chair closer to her. "Please have a seat."

She lowered herself onto the front edge of the chair, not sure what he had planned. But she was glad that Charles would be there soon.

The officer sat on the corner of the desk. "What were you looking for in the garden?"

A silly question. "What does one normally look for in a garden? Flowers."

He arched one eyebrow high on his forehead. "Cheeky, aren't you?"

"For stating the obvious?"

At the hurried knock on the open door, Charles looked up from the papers in front of him. Private Somers stood in the doorway. "First Lieutenant Young wants to see you immediately, sir."

What could Brantley want that was so urgent? Had something happened to Melissa? "Is he at home?"

"No, his office."

That confused Charles, but he stood and followed the marine.

At the doorway, he stopped and stood at attention. Brantley leaned against the corner of his desk. And at the periphery of his vision, Charles could see that some-one sat in a chair. He kept his gaze on his superior officer.

"Come in and close the door." Brantley motioned to-ward the person in the chair. "We have a situation here."

That was all Charles needed in the way of permission. As he shifted to close the door, he glanced at the person but stopped. "Rachel?"

She gave him a bright smile.

Brantley ordered, "Close the door."

Charles did. "What is she doing here?"

"Apparently, smelling flowers."

Rachel spoke up. "I wasn't smelling them."

The brothers glanced at her and then back at each other.

Charles spoke. "We have to get her out of here before the captain sees her."

"No. We have to take her to the captain. Too many of the men have seen her. He will learn she was here. Again."

Charles took a deep breath. "I'll take her."

"No, you won't. I will. It's best if you aren't seen with her."

"Then why did you send for me?"

"I thought you should know she had been here."

"May I speak with her? Alone?"

"Only for a moment." Brantley stepped outside but left the door ajar.

Charles knelt in front of Rachel. "What were you thinking, coming down the hill?"

"I wanted to see the flowers before they were all gone. I waited until everyone had moved inside for tea."

"Evidently not everyone."

"Evidently. I wasn't trying to get caught. What will your captain do with me?"

"Talk to you. And get you out of camp as fast as possible."

Brantley stepped back in. "I need to take her."

Charles stood and helped Rachel to her feet.

"You look as though I'm going to my execution."

Charles relaxed his shoulders. "No harm will come to you."

"Then why do you look so glum?"

"I can't say the same for me." He led her out and followed behind his brother.

"You won't get in trouble on my account, will you? You had nothing to do with me being here."

"But I did last time."

"He found out about that?"

"One can hardly keep a secret in such a small camp."

Brantley stopped at the captain's closed door. "Wait here." He knocked.

"Enter."

Brantley took a deep breath before turning the knob. He left the door open as he disappeared inside.

"What is it?"

"We have a situation, sir," Brantley said.

Rachel had certainly caused a *situation*.

"What?"

"It seems an American has wandered into camp."

"It is unlikely an American found himself here by accident. Bring him in."

"Sir—"

"I'll deal with him. Send him in."

Brantley appeared and gave Charles a look that told him to stay put. He motioned for Rachel to enter. She did.

"What's this?" Captain Bazalgette barked.

"The American, sir. Her name is Rachel Thompson."

"Is that your brother outside the door?"

"Yes, sir."

"Lieutenant Young, get in here!"

Charles took a deep breath and stepped into the captain's office. He stood at attention.

The captain scowled. "Is this the same girl you held here a while back?"

He hadn't held her. Why did the captain insist on wording it that way? "Yes, sir."

The captain turned his gaze back on Rachel. "Miss Thompson, are you trying to incite this war?"

She didn't flinch or cower. "No. Sir." The *sir* seemed to be an afterthought. She didn't have to address the captain as sir. He wasn't her commanding officer.

"Then what are you doing in my camp?"

"I wanted to look at the flowers in the garden. There are some I haven't seen before. And I have never seen such a garden. The little rows of bushes around all the beds. But the flowers are all gone for the winter."

The captain's eyes widened in surprise, whether from the simplicity and innocence of her answer or her forthrightness. "You would risk war over flowers?"

"I don't see how flowers could start a war."

"But a young lady unaccompanied in the opposition's camp could."

Rachel shrugged. "I won't tell if you won't."

Brantley choked on a laugh. Charles also had difficulty containing his mirth.

Captain Bazalgette glared briefly at the two of them, then focused back on Rachel. "You expect me to believe you came here simply to look at flowers and won't tell anyone that you've been here?"

"Why should I tell anyone? I didn't last time. You know about last time."

"Yes, young lady, I do. How do I know that you didn't intentionally get caught and American soldiers are just waiting to accuse us of misdeeds, giving them a reason to attack?"

"I didn't get caught on purpose. I waited until everyone went inside for tea. Well, I guess *everyone* hadn't gone in, after all."

Charles could tell that the captain didn't think Rachel was up to anything treacherous.

"I could lock you up for trespassing."

She squared her shoulders. "I don't think that would keep the peace."

Was his commanding officer trying to scare Rachel? It wasn't working. Either that or Rachel was hiding her fear. He didn't think so. Rachel knew the captain didn't want things to get out of hand.

"I'm going to let you go—this time. I don't ever want to see you back in my camp. If I catch you here again, I will throw you in my brig. Am I clear?"

"Yes, sir."

Charles could almost hear Rachel's following thought that she would make sure not to get caught next time. He couldn't imagine Rachel staying away.

"I'll have a wagon hitched and an escort take you home."

"You can't do that. I need to leave now. I've been away too long as it is. I can find my own way. If your soldiers go anywhere near my home, my papa *will* get this war riled up." Rachel turned and gave Charles a pleading look.

He wasn't sure what he could say. Speaking at all would upset his superior, but he didn't want Rachel to feel abandoned by him. "Sir?" he asked in a firm voice.

"Not a word from you."

At least Rachel would know he'd tried.

Captain Bazalgette glowered down at Rachel.

Charles watched his commanding officer as his expression made a minute shift in understanding. He, too, realized that if Rachel's father found out she was here, this could all end very badly. Or rather begin badly and get worse.

"You won't ever return?" the captain asked.

"No, sir."

"My officers will escort you part of the way."

"But—"

"No arguments. Go, before I change my mind." The captain motioned for Charles and his brother to see her off the premises.

"Thank you." Rachel turned and walked out with them.

Once outside, Charles said, "I'll see her the rest of the way."

"No. The captain ordered both of us, so I'm going, too."

Rachel led them up the hill. At the top, she tried to dismiss them, but Charles wouldn't let her. He needed to see her most of the way home and did.

Not too close to her house, Rachel said, "You should both turn back now."

Charles nodded to Brantley.

"I'll wait over there for you." Brantley walked off.

Charles stood in front of Rachel. "You can't ever come back down into the camp."

"I know." She held out her hands. "They stopped shaking."

"Your hands were shaking?"

"I thought your captain was going to put me in jail."

He smiled. "You could have fooled me. You called his bluff."

"Well, I didn't think he really wanted to start the war up. And you said he would let me go."

Rachel was so refreshing.

He bowed. "Goodbye, Rachel. 'Parting is such sweet sorrow.'" He left her there and met up with his brother.

Brantley nudged him with his shoulder. "I can see why she fascinates you. I thought she might start giving the captain orders."

She was a special young lady.

Charles crouched in some thick underbrush near Rachel's home. Her brother and three little sisters were in the yard, but Rachel wasn't around. And she was the one he'd hoped to catch a glimpse of.

Lindley looked straight at him, but he doubted the boy could actually see him. Then the boy meandered off around the house. Soon he could hear the boy coming through the woods. He moved to a different location. When Lindley thrust his stick sword at the bush he'd been hiding in, Charles came up behind him and used his own stick to poke his arm. "Put your hands up."

Lindley spun around. "How did you know I was coming?"

"You looked suspicious when you left the yard, and then you made noise coming through the trees."

Lindley slumped his shoulders in defeat.

"Now tell me how you knew I was here? I was sure you couldn't see me."

He tipped his head back and pointed up.

The boy wasn't saying that God had told him, was he? Charles looked up.

In the large fir tree nearby, Rachel waved to him.

He wanted to call up to her but didn't dare inform the rest of the household that he was present, so he turned to Lindley. "How long has she been up there?"

Lindley shrugged. "It's an easy tree to climb. The branches start low and go all the way up."

He noticed that Rachel was almost down. "You always climb trees in dresses?"

"Only when strange men are sneaking up to our home." She turned to Lindley. "Go back to the house."

"I want to stay here with the leftenant."

Just then a woman called out to them.

Rachel gripped Lindley's shoulder. "That's our mother. We both have to go." She pierced Charles with a glare. "You need to go, as well."

He watched her leave. Now he knew a bit of how she felt overlooking the camp. Like him, she probably never thought she would get caught. Yet they both had.

Chapter 10

For the next two and a half weeks, Rachel went to the overlook of English Camp every day that her siblings were in school. It was easy to break away in the afternoons when Genevieve took a nap with Priscilla.

Charles had gotten into the routine as well, and evidently knew when to meet her each day. He'd taken to bringing a blanket for them to sit upon.

"Why do you keep coming back here?" Rachel asked.

Charles eyed her for a moment, some sort of conflict playing on his expression. "Why do *you* keep coming back?"

She hesitated. "To see the garden in each of its seasons."

"The garden. Is that the only reason?"

"Of course. Anything else would be improper."

"Improper indeed."

She would try again. "So why do you keep coming back?"

A smile tugged at his lips. "The garden."

* * *

He watched her go. He liked watching her. Liked it a lot. "My dear sweet Rachel, what are you doing to me? You consume my every waking thought and even invade my dreams. I can't seem to get you out of my head. Not that I want to or that I have even tried. You are the song in my heart, the smile upon my lips, the hope for a future bright."

Now who was being dramatic? Rachel must be wearing off on him.

As long as he declared nothing and didn't allow his fingers to brush against hers even accidently, he could keep control of his disobedient longings. As it was, the memory haunted him of their first meeting, when he'd caught her from tumbling backward down the hill, and then later, when he'd taken her hand and bowed over it. He reveled in reliving those moments, even while he tried to forget what it had felt like to have his hands about her waist or her soft, delicate hand in his.

She was both intoxicating and sobering. She was American. He English. Their peoples were at war. On opposite sides.

His Romeo to her Juliet.

Neither the play nor war ever ended well.

The following week, Rachel sat with her back against a large tree. Charles had brought the blanket and found a place they could sit where no one was likely to stumble across them.

Charles faced her, his hip nearly touching her own, the closest he'd ever sat to her. His nearness made her heart skip a beat. He hadn't touched her or attempted to touch her since that first day when he prevented her from falling on the hill and then bowed over her hand as they parted.

"Continue reading," Charles encouraged her. "I like your accent."

Rachel smiled. "I don't have an accent. You do."

"You have one to me. Please continue. I like the way you read. You have passion. You read with a fresh perspective that comes out in your voice."

"How can you hear a perspective in my voice?"

"In the emphasis you give certain words and syllables. You don't just read the piece. You experience it."

Amazing. That was just how she felt when she read the poetry, as though she was transported into the world of the poem.

The earthy smell of forest mixing with the salty air was a heady, intoxicating scent. And Charles's nearness intensified it.

"Are you going to continue or would you like me to read?"

She did love to hear his accent. "Close your eyes." Her heart sped up at the decision she'd just made.

He narrowed his eyes. "Why? What are you about?"

"Is a trained military officer afraid of little ol' me?"

"Small, unassuming things can sometimes be the most dangerous."

"Am I seeing fear in your eyes?"

They twinkled. "Curiosity."

Having second thoughts, she turned back to the book and slid her finger down the page to find her place. "A curiosity that will never be satisfied."

He held out his hands, palms up. "Very well. I place my life in your hands." He closed his eyes.

"The moment has passed." She didn't look up from the book.

"I will keep my eyes closed until…until you do whatever you were going to do."

She was too self-conscious now. "Ah, here is where I

was. 'And then he took the cross divine, / Where the sun shines fair on Carlisle wall, / And died for her sake in Palestine; / So Love was still the lord of all.'" She hesitated and dared to glance at him. His eyes were still closed.

He continued the poem. "'Now all ye lovers, that faithful prove, / (The sun shines fair on Carlisle wall,)...'"

She gazed at him while he recited the last verse.

He spoke with passion and emotion. "'Pray for their souls who died for love, / For Love shall still be lord of all!'"

Her favorite *Romeo and Juliet* quotation went through her mind. *See, how she leans her cheek upon her hand! / O, that I were a glove upon that hand, / That I might touch that cheek!* Her courage renewed, she laid her hand upon his cheek.

He sucked in a breath and pressed into her hand while covering hers with his warm one, but he kept his eyes closed.

She hoped he didn't push her away. His touch gave her the continued courage to move forward. She could feel the heat of his breath a moment before she touched his lips with hers.

He leaned into her, returning her kiss with ardor, and placed his other hand upon her cheek.

After a moment, he pulled back and rested his forehead against hers. "You should not have done that."

"Why?" Had she done it wrong? She had no experience in such things.

"I will find it impossible to stay away from you now. I knew as long as I didn't cross that physical boundary and touch you, I could somehow let you go when the time came."

So it had been a conscious choice to keep his distance. Let her go? When the time came?

"Now I can never let you go." He kissed her this time.

And she enjoyed it.

He broke the kiss. "Marry me."

"What? No." She stood and backed away. "Impossible." Papa would never allow it. She hadn't let herself even think it.

He stared up at her. "Not exactly what a man wants to hear from his lady love."

"Love? You can't possibly love me."

"But I do." He stood and took her hands. "I'm sure you have affection for me, as well."

Of course she held affection for him, but that was beside the point. Shaking her head, she pulled her hands free. "I can't."

He looked wounded. "Then why did you kiss me?"

"I don't know."

"Have you been trifling with my affections, Miss Thompson?"

"No. Yes. No. Maybe. I don't know!" She supposed she could have been. She knew nothing could really have become of their meetings…their friendship…their relationship. If she could find an American man who had his qualities, who would allow her to be herself, he would be perfect. But no man or woman was perfect.

He took her hands again. "Tell me you care at least a little, even in a small way. Anything." Now he sounded as dramatic as she.

She whispered, "If I speak of my feelings aloud, they will become real. If they become real, I can no longer pretend they don't exist. If they exist, then I will feel them. And the pain of unrequited feelings will be too much to bear."

"Your feelings won't be unrequited. I lo—"

Rachel put her fingers on his lips. She couldn't let him say it, or the pain in their parting would be too great.

He kissed her fingers. "I love you."

She pulled her hand away. The words rose unbidden in her throat. "I—" She stopped and looked away. "I never imagined you would come to hold affection for me."

"Why not?"

"I am but a country girl. You are a naval officer. I am simple. You are sophisticated." She dropped her voice. "I am American. You are—"

"Don't say the enemy."

"English."

"We English have feelings, too."

"But I'm an American."

"Still not an answer."

"You're in the military."

"So I have no feelings? How could I resist you? I was at your mercy from the first moment I met you. I tried to stay away but could not. I tried to remain aloof but could not. I tried to think of you as just a friend but could not. It cut my heart and left it bleeding to think of your father looking for a husband for you and knowing he would never consider me as a potential suitor. Thinking of you in another man's arms."

"But you aren't the one who kissed me. You never even touch me. Even accidently. Since that first day."

"Because I knew if I did, I would be hopelessly lost to you. I knew it wouldn't be fair to you. I didn't let myself hope that you were returning for anything more than to read the books."

The books were the smallest part of why she returned. "The garden." She had made a mess of things.

He smiled. "Yes, the garden. When was the last time you even glanced at it?"

Weeks.

He took her hand and pressed it to his chest over his heart. "I came to these islands specifically to avoid any kind of entanglements with a lady. I had no desire ever to marry after seeing my brothers' unhappy matches. But I know you are nothing like their wives."

She could feel his strong heartbeat thumping under her palm. Her eyes burned. She blinked, and a tear slipped out.

He raised his other hand and, with his thumb, he caressed away the tear from her cheek.

She leaned into his touch. "I'm sorry."

"Don't be. I'm glad to know you return my affections."

She stepped away, breaking his hold. "I can't."

"But you already do," he insisted. "Even if I wanted to, which I don't, I couldn't change how I feel about you. Can you?"

"I have to."

"Once a bird has soared in the sky, it will never be content in the nest again." He held out his hand for her to take. "I will figure a way."

She stared at his hand. "How? Papa will never let you court me."

"Maybe when the island dispute is settled, he won't have an issue with us English."

"How will the dispute be settled? War? Bloodshed?"

"I don't know."

"How long? The war has already been going on for more than ten years. Another ten years? This war will never be over."

"There is talk of possibly getting an arbitrator to settle the matter."

"Talk? Possibly?"

He held his hand a little closer to her. "Trust me."

Him she trusted. It was the rest of the world. *What should I do, Lord?*

"Please."

Slowly, she placed her hand on his.

He wrapped his fingers around hers and pulled her close. "I'll find a way."

She leaned against his chest in his warm embrace, believing he could.

Charles didn't know whether he could make this all work out for them, but he knew he had to do something. He couldn't imagine not having Rachel in his life. He wanted to test the depth of her feelings for him, so he closed the gap between them, cupped her face in his hands and captured her mouth with his.

Though she seemed unpracticed, she didn't push him away. Instead, she hooked her arms around to his back with one hand on each of his shoulders.

Encouraged, he slipped his arms around her and deepened the kiss, tangling his fingers in the silky, ebony hair hanging down her back.

She molded into his embrace and sighed contentedly.

He kissed her more thoroughly.

He had kissed ladies before, since he was a schoolboy, but no kiss had been as satisfying as this, with Rachel. And he realized why. This was the first time his heart had ever been involved.

Rachel pulled away from him. "I have to go."

He held on to her hand. "You'll come back?"

"I don't know."

"If you don't, I'll come to your house again."

"No! You mustn't. That's too dangerous." Her blue, blue eyes beseeched him.

"No more dangerous than you coming here. You shouldn't have to traipse through the forest. I'm the gentleman. I should be calling on you."

"Papa would run you off with his musket. Promise you won't come to my house."

He knew she was right that it was less likely they would be discovered meeting here, rather than near her house. But he would gladly risk the trip to see her again. Before today, he would have accepted it if she'd told him she would never see him again or asked him to go away.

But that kiss had changed everything.

"Promise you'll come back. I have to know I'll see you again."

She nodded.

But he wasn't so sure. "I meant what I said. I do love you."

"I…I…"

He put his finger on her lips. "Don't say anything. It's all right." He kissed her forehead. "Go. I'll see you soon."

She wrapped her arms around him, giving him a quick hug before running off.

He watched her moving quickly through the underbrush, not once looking back. *Lord, I have to see her again.*

Even though she had kissed him first, he knew it would have been only a matter of time before his will broke and he kissed her. Hadn't that been evident in how close he'd sat to her today? And faced her? If he'd had any will at all left, he would have pushed her away instead of drawing closer and kissing her as he had. And the feel of her silky hair in his fingers. Better than he'd imagined. The game he'd been playing had suddenly become real.

Brantley was right. He wouldn't risk everything for a woman who was *just* a friend. He wouldn't have to. But for the woman he loved, he would. Not much else seemed to matter without Rachel now that he knew how she felt about him. Except the Lord.

God, what should I do? How do I get Rachel's father to accept me?

The word honor *popped into his head.*
Honor.
He would act honorably. But what exactly did that mean in this situation?

Chapter 11

Rachel ran through the woods. She couldn't tell whether she was running away from her feelings for Charles, or simply running home. But she couldn't stop. She had never meant to care for him. And she certainly never meant to have him care for her. No. More than care. He'd said he loved her. She never imagined he felt so strongly for her.

Did she love him, too? Her heart screamed, *Yes!* But she hadn't let herself think that could be possible. She just thought he saw her as a silly girl who read romance stories and trudged through the forest to peer at a fancy garden.

When she neared her home, she stopped and leaned against a tree to catch her breath. She remembered the feel of his warm lips on hers. He hadn't laughed at her or called her silly. He'd said he loved her! And proposed marriage! She thrilled at the idea. To have Charles to herself and not have to slip through the forest in hopes of seeing him. The garden indeed. She hadn't even thought of it in a long while. Not even the books could draw her there so much. It had been Charles for weeks.

Perhaps from the first day.

But could Charles really change Papa's mind? Could Papa ever see Charles as an honorable man first and an Englishman second? Yes, maybe he could. At least she hoped so.

Taking one final deep breath, she pushed away from the tree and headed for the house.

Lindley met her before she broke through the tree line at the backyard. "Papa's looking for you."

"You didn't tell him where you thought I was, did you?"

"I'm not a dunce."

No, he wasn't. He seemed to enjoy Charles's company almost as much as she did. She smoothed her hands down her skirt and broke out from the trees.

Papa marched toward her. "Where have you been?"

"I was walking in the woods. Genevieve said I could go." Could Papa hear her pounding heart? It raced from the exertion of running. It raced from fear of being found out. And it raced from the memory of Charles's kisses and the feel of his arms around her.

Papa drew in a long breath. "As long as you are all right. I just worry when I don't know where you are. I wish you wouldn't go off so long alone."

"I'm fine, Papa."

"Your mother liked the woods, as well."

Papa never spoke of Mama. When he did mention her, Rachel could see pain in his eyes.

"Henry Olson is waiting to take you on a buggy ride."

She stared at Papa a moment, sorting out the meaning of his words. Henry Olson, the suitor with orange hair, attacked by freckles. And she was supposed to be letting him court her. She didn't want to go. Not now that she'd freed her feelings for Charles. "Papa, I look a mess." She held out her skirt from her sides.

"Where is this vanity coming from? You look quite suitable."

"Mr. Olson is nice, but I don't fancy him as a suitor. I tried, truly I did."

"Nonsense. Try harder. You will go on a buggy ride with him, and you will be cordial."

She would honor Papa's wishes, but she would never feel for Henry Olson what she felt for Charles.

Papa ushered her inside, where Henry sat conversing with Genevieve in the parlor. Papa had found a man whom she hadn't rejected out of hand, and he was going to insist on this one.

Rachel's stomach knotted.

Henry Olson stood. "Miss Thompson, you look especially lovely." The few minuscule patches of skin between all the spots filled in red.

"Thank you, Mr. Olson."

"I would consider it an honor if you would call me Henry."

"Of course, Henry. And you may call me Rachel." She hoped that would make Papa happy.

Henry's skin patches darkened, and he held out his elbow to her.

She took it and went out to his buggy. He gave her a hand up and climbed in after her. He set the buggy into motion, and they rode in silence. She didn't know what to say, so she smiled at him, and he smiled back.

Finally she said, "Do you like to read?" Maybe she could find something to talk about with him.

"I don't have time."

So she couldn't talk about books with him. "If you had the time, would you like to read?"

"I don't think so."

That ended that topic.

She wished he would pick something to talk about, but he didn't.

"What do you think of the English?"

"They're fine."

She waited for him to say more, but he didn't.

"Fine? How so?"

He shrugged. "Just, fine."

She couldn't accuse him of being verbose. Was there even any point in trying to start another conversation?

Silence filled the rest of the ride.

Painful silence.

When at last he looped the buggy back around to her house, he helped her out.

"Thank you. The buggy ride was delightful."

Papa came out. "Henry, won't you come inside?"

Henry dipped his head. "I need to be getting back." He turned to her. "Thank you, Rachel. I had a nice time. Good afternoon." He climbed aboard his buggy and left.

Papa said, "Henry is a good man."

"Papa, I couldn't even have a conversation with him. He didn't want to talk. I know he's nice, but please don't make me see him again."

"You could do a lot worse than a man like Henry. And if I say he can court you, then you will be nice to him."

Genevieve stood in the doorway.

Rachel gave her a pleading look. "You understand."

"Obey your father." Contrary to her stepmother's words, Rachel could see compassion in her eyes.

Later that evening, when everyone had gone to bed, Rachel got up to go to the outhouse. On her way back, she could hear Papa and Genevieve talking in their room. Papa asked, "What do you think of Henry Olson?"

"As you said, he is a good man."

"But?"

"But I cannot see Rachel married to him."

"Why not?"

"She is spirited. Henry is too timid. She would never be happy."

"I know. It's not easy finding a man worthy of my daughter."

Rachel tiptoed back into her room, elated. Papa wouldn't make her endure poor Henry again. She did hope Henry found a nice, quiet girl to marry who would make him happy. She was sure he would not be happy with her.

Her heart belonged to Charles.

When she'd dreamed of having her own Romeo, she had been thinking only of the part where the man of her dreams loved her deeply. She hadn't even considered the forbidden part. She'd never wanted that. But that was exactly what she had.

"You saw her again, didn't you?"

Charles didn't want to lie to his brother, but neither did he want to answer him.

Brantley gripped his shoulders. "You'd better be sure she is worth it, little brother."

Oh, she was. If he'd been asked three months ago, before he met Rachel, he would have said there wasn't a woman in all the world who could make him give up anything, let alone everything. But now he was considering just that.

"I envy you."

He wasn't sure what his brother meant. "How so?"

"To be in love. Something our brothers and I were not afforded."

"What makes you think I'm in love?"

"You continue to take risks to see her. You are playing with fire. You are going to get burned one way or another. Or she will. Or both of you."

Right now Charles felt as though he could conquer anything. Even bridge the gap between two warring countries.

Then the unbidden thought of this war erupting turned his stomach. Peace had to remain. If he faced Rachel's father on the battlefield...what? What would he do? Desert? Never.

He would lay down his arms and beg her father to take him captive. That would be better than the man killing him. If that happened and Rachel found out, she might not forgive her father. And Charles certainly wouldn't knowingly kill her father.

He was in quite a pickle.

Chapter 12

Charles watched Rachel's house from partway up the large tree she had climbed before. He felt like a boy again up here. He caught a glimpse of her through one of the windows, and his pulse sped up. He strained to see her again but couldn't unless she moved near a window.

She hadn't come to the camp yesterday or the day before. He needed to see her. Needed to know whether she'd changed her mind about him or she truly cared for him. Before the kisses they'd shared, he had been prepared to let her go, as hard as that might be. But now the thought of a life without her caused a grief deep in his soul.

Since confessing his love for her, that feeling had unfolded and swaddled him in a protective cocoon. Loving her felt right. As though it was always meant to be. The reason the Lord had brought him to these islands. He'd thought he'd been running away from taking a wife. He didn't know the Lord had been leading him to her. The thought of taking a wife before had nauseated him. Now the thought of not having Rachel for his wife caused his insides to knot up in pain. He took several deep breaths to uncoil them.

He loved her. And would continue to love her until the day he died. She was the one God intended for him. The one he would do anything for. The one he would die for. The one forbidden to him. Just like Romeo.

He had always thought that men who acted like Romeo—and now like himself—were fools. Worse than fools. Vacuous. Women weren't worth a man losing himself over. But now he understood. As weak as love made a man, it also made him stronger. He felt he could conquer anything, take on the world. Even bridge warring countries. Or tame her father's feelings about the English.

But when Rachel hadn't returned, he'd doubted her feelings for him, and he hadn't slept well last night. He feared he'd frightened her off. It was still a little early in the day for her to show up at the camp. He just hoped she would come out of the house and move far enough away from it for him to approach her.

She stepped through the doorway with her coat on and trudged straight away from the house toward the trees, with purpose in her steps.

Could that purpose be him? He prayed so.

Uncertain how she would receive him, he remained in the tree. She passed and kept going without looking up. Why would she? She appeared to be heading in the direction of camp. He would follow her a bit to make sure.

When she stopped suddenly, he ducked behind a large sword fern. After a few moments, she continued. Then she stopped again. "Who's there?"

Caught. He stepped out from hiding. "Just me."

Her eyes widened, and she smiled.

As he walked forward, he held his arms out, and she rushed into them.

"What are you doing here? You promised not to come here. It's too dangerous."

"I came to see you." He cupped her face in his hands. "I got worried when you didn't come the last two days."

"Priscilla's been ill. I haven't been able to get away."

"Then I didn't scare you off with my declaration of love."

"Of course not. I love you, too."

His heart soared. He claimed her lips with his own.

Kissing him back, she slipped her arms around him.

He had wondered if she felt the same for him. She hadn't said so the other day, and he'd been eaten up inside not knowing. He pulled back but still held her in his arms. "You didn't answer my question the other day."

"What question?"

He loosened his hold and slid his hands down her arms to take her hands as he lowered to one knee. "Will you do me the great honor and privilege of being my wife?"

"Truly, you want to marry me?"

"Most definitely. Did you think I was trifling with you?"

A conflict warred in her expression.

"Please say you want to be my wife."

"I do. I just don't see how it would be possible. Papa will never allow it. And I doubt your commander will either."

He stood, keeping hold of her hands. "The captain wouldn't mind as long as it didn't cause this war to erupt." On the other hand, his parents, half a world away, wouldn't be pleased with him marrying an American. At least not one with no social standing. "We could run off and secretly marry just like Romeo and Juliet."

"That didn't end well for either of them."

How true. "If you appear to have met your demise, I

will sit at your side until you awaken and promise to resist the urge to plunge a knife into my gut."

"And I promise not to take poison. More than likely, if we ran off secretly, the war our marriage would fuel would be the end of one or both of us."

Yes, the war that wasn't would always stand between them as long as they were on opposite sides. "I'll quit the military if it will make your father less averse to me."

She pushed away from him. "What? You can't do that. Don't you come from a long line of military people?"

"Yes, but if that's what it will take to be with you, I will give up everything."

"You would do that for me?"

"Most certainly."

"I can't let you."

"You can't stop me. If I'm not an English officer, your father will have fewer qualms about me."

"But you will still be English."

Yes, that would still be the problem. How did he stop being the nationality he was born into? He adopted an American accent. "Then I'll be American."

Rachel giggled.

He continued with his new accent. "What? Can't I pass for American? Isn't my accent good enough?"

"You sound like an Englishman trying very hard to sound like an American."

It was his brother Prescott who could talk like other people. "Do you think you can do any better putting on an English accent?"

She conjured up what he guessed was her best imitation. "I do believe an English accent is something I can muster."

He smiled. "Not too bad. I'd say somewhere north, perhaps Cumbria in the Carlisle area."

She smiled at her victory.

He gazed at her. She was so beautiful when she smiled. "I have never seen a lovelier lady than thee."

She blushed. "I'm sure that's not true. You likely have a hundred young ladies waiting for your return."

"Nay. But if I did, every last one of them would be disappointed. My heart belongs to thee, my lady love."

Later in the day, after Rachel had turned her insides around with worry, she returned to English Camp and waited. But not at her usual overlook. She was about to give up when she saw Charles's brother and tracked his movement across the grounds. He went toward the area Charles had said was the officers' housing. She approached the path he was on. No one else seemed to be around, so she moved from her hiding place.

Charles's brother saw her, stopped and looked around. Then he came over to her. "You shouldn't be here." He guided her around a cabin and into the trees. He faced her. "Do you want Charles to get stripped of his rank?"

"No. That's why I'm here."

"What?"

"Charles said that he is going to leave the military so we can be together. I can't let him do that. You have to talk to him." She couldn't let him give up everything when he would likely get nothing for his efforts. Papa would *never* accept him.

"My brother has a will of his own."

"I won't see him anymore. I won't come back. Tell him that. Tell him to leave me alone."

Charles's brother smiled. "I can see why my baby brother is so enthralled with you."

"What? Why?"

"Besides being quite pleasant on the eyes, witty and charming, you are selfless."

She was not selfless. She often thought of herself. She

read whenever she got the chance. When she wanted to see the fancy garden at English Camp, she snuck off. When she wanted to see Charles, she snuck off. "I can attest to the fact that I'm quite selfish."

"If you were selfish, you would grab hold of my brother and take advantage of his social standing and money."

That didn't make any sense. "But he's just a soldier."

Charles's brother laughed. "He is not *just a soldier.* He is an officer in Her Majesty's British Royal Navy. Do you know what that means?"

Since she thought he *was* just a soldier—well, an officer—she obviously didn't know what that meant, but it sounded impressive when his brother added Her Majesty's British Royal Navy. She shook her head.

"It means he comes from a family of privilege. We may not be nobility with titles, but we are gentry."

Gentry? That sounded fancy.

"They don't let just any bloke be an officer, unlike you Americans."

"Honestly, I don't know how either military works."

"And now that you know Charles has money, rank and a high social standing, would you like to reconsider walking out of his life? Of course, he could lose it all if he takes up with you. As well as ignite this war into an uncontrollable inferno."

She couldn't let any of that happen, and she certainly wouldn't fit in with the kind of people Charles was used to. "You have to convince him to stay away from me. Do whatever you have to do to make him understand that it will never work. That we will both be unhappy."

"I'll do my best, but I won't make any promises."

"You have to convince him. You have to."

Charles picked at the bark of a fir tree. His brother had made a strange request. Meet him on the far side of camp, away from the water that could carry their voices far and wide. He'd made his way to the meeting place and waited. Brantley eventually arrived.

Charles remained leaning against the large tree. He loved the massive size of the trees here. They reminded him of England. "What's this all about? Why the secrecy?"

"Your lady love came to see me."

His insides tumbled at the thought of Rachel. He couldn't admit there was anything between them, so he acted nonchalant. "What lady?"

Brantley gripped his shoulder. "Brother, I know your secret. Rachel came to me about you. She doesn't want to see you again. She doesn't want you to lose or give up everything because of her. She said she wasn't coming back. She wants you to forget about her."

"I could never forget about her. I've tried."

Brantley released him and shrugged. "And I tried to dissuade you, too. You'll tell her so, won't you?"

His brother was confusing. "You didn't try very hard."

"I like her. She's cheeky. A spirited young lady. When I told her you had money and social standing, she was more determined to cut you free."

"My death is the only thing that can free me, she has so completely settled herself in my heart."

Brantley clapped a hand on Charles's shoulder. "You won't find another lady like her even if you grow to be a very old man. You should hold on to her."

"Even if it sets fire to this war?"

"Well, the way you are going about it, you just might."

"What are you suggesting?"

"Honor."

There was that word again. He stared at his brother. "I have not behaved dishonorably with Rachel."

"Haven't you?"

"No!" How dare his brother even suggest such a thing?

"Sneaking around behind everyone's backs? That is hardly honorable, little brother."

Brantley was right. If Charles wanted Rachel, he had to win over her father first, and to do that, he needed to start behaving honorably on all fronts. "How do I ingratiate myself to a man who hates me for the country I was born into?"

"How indeed?"

His brother was going to be of little help.

Chapter 13

After the children had left for school, Rachel sat by the window, looking out. Gray clouds hung heavy in the sky, like her guilt hung heavy in her heart. She hadn't gone to English Camp in a week. Each day she feared Charles might show up at their farm. But so far she hadn't seen him. That didn't mean he hadn't been there without revealing himself. His brother must have made him see reason. But her desire to finish the book of poems was calling to her today.

Genevieve sat with Priscilla at the table, feeding the nine-month-old mashed potatoes. "What's wrong, Rachel?"

"Nothing."

"Well, you have something weighing on your mind." Suddenly, her stepmother stood next to her with Priscilla on her hip.

Rachel obviously hadn't been paying attention to what Genevieve was doing. "I'm fine. Do you need me to do something for you? Take Prissy?"

"I've got her. It's a young man, isn't it?"

"What?"

"I have watched you moping around the house for a week now. You're in love, aren't you?"

She didn't know it could be so painful. Or so obvious. But she couldn't admit it, not even to Genevieve, who was often on her side in affairs of the heart.

"You don't have to tell me. I know by the look in your eyes. Your father is reasonable. As long as this man is a good, God-fearing man, I don't see him having any objections."

Oh, but Papa would.

"Tell me who he is, and I'll hint to your father that he should bring him over for supper." She made it sound so simple.

Invite him over, and Papa would welcome an English officer—the enemy—into his family. More likely, he would shoot Charles.

"I can't." Rachel pulled in her bottom lip and bit down hard to keep from crying.

"I can't think of anyone your father wouldn't agree to you courting. Except—" Genevieve stared at her. "Rachel, say it isn't so. Not an Englishman?"

Rachel's eyes teared up. "I never meant to."

"You have to stop seeing him at once."

"That's what I've been doing. You aren't going to tell Papa, are you?"

Genevieve shook her head. "But you must forget about this man."

"I'm trying, but I can't."

"Try harder, or your father will take notice of your demeanor." Genevieve turned to the baby. "I need to put a dry diaper on Priscilla. I'll be right back, and we'll talk more about this." She went to the other room.

Rachel didn't want to talk about it anymore. It would only make matters worse. She shrugged on her coat and hurried out the door.

Before she knew where she was headed, her feet—or her heart—had taken her to English Camp. She stopped short and hid.

Missing Charles so much, she ached inside. And today, it had gotten the better of her. Here she was at the very place she said she'd stay away from. But she had come at a time she normally didn't, so Charles shouldn't be here.

She stayed in hiding for a while to make sure Charles was nowhere around. Though she wanted to see him, she knew it wasn't wise. She had accepted that she would never see him again. She couldn't.

She went to the secret place under the edge of the log and pulled out the three books. She wanted to read them all, but mostly wanted to finish the poetry. So she set the other two books aside and unwrapped the poems. On the cover of the book was a folded sheet of paper.

Her heart sped up, knowing the note had to be from Charles. Reluctant to see what he wrote, she closed her eyes and took a deep breath. Then she opened her eyes and unfolded the paper.

My Dearest Rachel,
I understand your concerns. But know that I have not given up on us. I will find a way for us to be together.
My heart is yours,
Charles

She pressed the letter to her chest. He hadn't given up. She hoped he could find a way.
Lord, please help him find a way.

* * *

Charles remained behind a tree, watching Rachel. He wanted to go to her. To hold her. To kiss her. But he knew he mustn't. That would not be the honorable thing. He just wasn't sure what the honorable thing was. How could he still end up with Rachel and not ignite this war? When she hugged his short letter, it nearly broke his resolve, but he remained hidden.

Lord, I love her so much. You know I never intended to fall in love. I was avoiding taking a wife, but You have placed this woman in my heart. I don't believe You would have brought us together if You didn't intend us ultimately to be together. Show me what I'm supposed to do.

The only thought that came to him was *patience.*

He had never considered himself a patient man.

Chapter 14

Once again, Papa urged Rachel to answer the knock on their door. She had hoped Papa had given up on finding her a husband. She couldn't very well refuse, or Genevieve might tell Papa about her feelings for the Englishman.

She opened the door and was surprised to see a man in uniform. An American army uniform.

Papa stood behind her. "This is Sergeant Hicks. Sergeant Hicks, my daughter Rachel."

Sergeant Hicks gave a stiff bow. "Pleased to meet you, Miss Rachel. Please call me Stanley."

Rachel tried to force a smile and hoped she succeeded. "Pleased to meet you…Stanley." Stanley might be a perfectly fine man with a lot of good qualities that she would have been highly attracted to at another time in her life. But she loved Charles, and she didn't see any other man changing that.

After supper, as they were all shuffling from the table, Rachel really wanted to help clear the table and to wash *and* dry the dishes. Anything to occupy her so she didn't have to force polite conversation with Stanley that would only lead him to think there could be anything real between them.

Winnie perched at the window. "A man's coming."

Alice ran to the window. "A soldier."

Lindley reached the window, as well.

"Get away from the window," Papa commanded them.

Lindley gave Rachel a pointed look as he obeyed Papa.

Papa and Stanley went to the window in tandem.

"A Brit." Papa spat out the word as though it were a curse. He went to the mantel and retrieved his musket.

Now Genevieve gave Rachel a stern look.

Stanley stepped between Papa and the door. "Sir, allow me to see what the lieutenant wants."

Papa stood eye to eye with the sergeant, neither man moving.

Lieutenant? *Yes, Papa, let Stanley go talk to him.* She wanted desperately to go to the window but didn't dare move lest Papa take his gun outside.

"Please, sir." Stanley measured his words and spoke with deliberateness and forcefulness. "We don't want this to get out of control. Let me handle it."

After a few deep breaths, Papa gave a quick nod.

Stanley exited.

Rachel went to the window as Charles dismounted. Stanley met him by his horse and shook his hand. They seemed to know each other.

"Rachel, get away from the window."

She moved back at Papa's order but could still see out. She wished she knew what they were saying.

Papa stepped up to the window, blocking her view. She shifted sideways to regain her line of sight.

Charles and Stanley conversed for several minutes. Then Charles held out a paper to Stanley. Stanley didn't take it right away, but after more words from Charles, he did.

Charles seemed to be explaining the paper.

What could it possibly be? Was it some sort of military document stating that the islands belonged to England, and if they wanted to stay, they would have to become English citizens? Were the English declaring war on the Americans? That didn't make sense. Why would Charles be delivering the message? And to her house? And how did he know an American soldier would be there? No. It had to be something else.

Soon Charles turned, mounted his horse and rode off.

Stanley returned inside, and now he gave her a look. Then he handed the paper to Papa. "This came for your daughter."

Rachel gasped and held her breath. Had the commanding officer decided to charge her with trespassing, after all?

Papa glanced from the paper to her and back. He unfolded it, and his expression went grave as he read. The muscle in his jaw worked back and forth, and his breathing became deliberate and controlled.

It must be something serious.

Stanley tipped his head in a slight bow. "I'll take my leave, sir. Thank you for supper." He gave Rachel a nod and left.

Ordinarily, she would have been glad he'd left, but tonight she wished he'd stayed.

Papa handed the paper to Genevieve. "Rachel, in the parlor. Children, go to your rooms."

Her insides tightened. This could not be good. She slowly went into the parlor and sat on the settee. She could hear the children scampering up the stairs.

Papa and Genevieve remained in the other room talking in low voices. Papa was not happy. The two finally came into the parlor. Genevieve sat in one of the chairs opposite her and gave Rachel a sympathetic look.

Papa paced. He was upset and trying to sort out his thoughts. He stared out the window.

Rachel wished he would just get on with it. But to tell him so would only upset him more.

After a few moments, Papa turned and held up the paper. "Do you know what this is?"

She couldn't even venture a guess. "No, Papa." But she was about to find out.

"It's an invitation to that absurd Christmas party the tyrannical English insist on throwing every year."

Rachel thrilled at being invited to the English Christmas party. She wanted to go, desperately so. Would Papa let them?

Papa continued, "We are at war, and they throw a party. No wonder we beat them in the Revolution. They don't take serious things seriously."

She could tell that Papa wasn't planning to attend the English party. Rachel wanted to say that she believed the English were trying to promote goodwill between the two sides, but Papa didn't want to hear that. She had to let him say whatever he wanted to say. Maybe she could convince him to go. Then he would see that Charles was a good man. "Isn't Christmas supposed to be a time of peace to put differences aside?"

Papa glared and pointed the paper at her. "Maybe you can tell me why an English officer has addressed an invitation to *you*?"

Oh, dear. Maybe they were asking all the young ladies and their families to attend? Even in her head it sounded implausible. And she reckoned Papa wasn't really wanting her to answer. He was telling her she had been caught.

"Have you somehow met one of the English officers?"

She had no choice but to confess. "When I was walking in the forest, I might have met one."

Papa raised an eyebrow. "*Might* have met one?"

Rachel glanced at Genevieve for support, but her stepmother sat impassive. She would side with her husband. As she should.

"Yes, Papa." Rachel looked down at her lap. "I met an English officer in the forest."

"You have disgraced this family."

"No, Papa. I didn't do anything wrong. We only talked and sometimes read from a book."

His eyes narrowed.

She hadn't meant to reveal so much.

"It sounds as though you have seen him on more than one occasion."

"Yes, Papa."

"This Lieutenant Young on the invitation?"

"Yes, Papa."

"You've been frolicking with the enemy behind my back? You know how I feel about the English. How could you do this?"

How indeed? "I didn't do it on purpose. I met him by accident."

"Over and over?"

Each time had been less accidental and more hopeful until she planned out how and when to see him. "Papa, he's not a bad man. He's a Christian."

"He's the enemy."

"He is not."

"You know how I feel about *them*."

"But I don't know why."

"I don't have to explain my actions to you. You are my daughter, and you will do as I see fit. I think maybe a husband will settle you. Someone who can handle your strong will."

"Papa, no."

"Henry Olson liked you. But you would rule him. Buck Anderson was strong-minded."

She would run away from him.

"Perhaps Sergeant Hicks."

Rachel didn't know how to beg for her freedom, so she clutched her hands to her chest and knelt. "'Good father, I beseech you on my knees, Hear me with patience but to speak a word.'"

Papa pulled down his eyebrows then turned to Genevieve. "What is she prating about?"

"I think she's quoting from one of her books."

"Get up," Papa commanded. "And stop all this nonsense."

Like Juliet's plea to her father, Rachel's had fallen on deaf ears. Tears filled her eyes as she pushed up from the floor. "May I go?"

Papa nodded.

She stood and walked from the room.

Papa called after her. "Rachel."

She turned back.

"You will *not* leave this house. Is that understood?"

She wanted to argue but knew it would do no good.

"I need your word."

She gave a small nod of consent.

As she turned away, she heard Papa say to Genevieve, "Maybe I should take her books away if this is how they are going to make her act."

Papa had spoken more for her benefit than to Genevieve. To let Rachel know just how displeased he was with her.

Genevieve replied, "Would it do any good when she has so much of them memorized?"

Rachel plodded up the stairs. *Lord, please cool Papa's*

anger and let him see reason. I desperately want to attend the Christmas party.

Lindley sat at the top of the stairs, waiting. He stood as she approached. "Why was the leftenant here?"

"He invited us all to the annual English Camp Christmas party."

"Really?" The excitement in her brother's voice was bittersweet. "Will Papa let us go?"

"No, Papa will not let us go, and I'm confined to the house."

"Why?"

"I had to tell him about meeting Charles."

To his credit, Lindley paled. "I'm sorry, Rachel. I liked seeing him."

So did she. More so than Lindley ever could.

Lindley grabbed her wrist and pulled her to his room. He looked both ways down the hall. Satisfied, he closed the door.

What was he up to this time?

"You write the leftenant a letter, and I'll take it to him."

Papa had confined *her* to the house but not Lindley. "You would do that for me? I would like to explain to him that we won't be coming to the party and not to expect any response from Papa."

"Sure."

Of course Lindley would do it. It would give him a reason to go on an adventure by himself. "I'll write it tonight and give it to you in the morning."

She went back to her room, pulled out *Romeo and Juliet*, and opened to the page with the pressed purple flower. Then she sat down to pen her letter.

Chapter 15

Charles stared at the report he was supposed to be writing. He was no further along on it than he had been an hour ago. His thoughts kept circling back to *why*? Why hadn't he heard anything from Rachel or her family about the party? The party was in less than a week, and he had delivered the invitation himself nearly a week ago.

The American sergeant had tried to talk him out of delivering the invitation. The sergeant knew that Rachel's father was a patriot. Charles had insisted, his way of making his intentions known. But not receiving a reply either way didn't bode well. If he had heard something, he would have known how to proceed, but now...? The silence was disconcerting. And unnerving.

Had the sergeant even turned over his invitation?

Charles had wondered why the sergeant was there. It was as though someone knew he was coming and had had the sergeant waiting. But he hadn't told anyone he was going that night. Late in the night as he'd wrestled with his covers, the answer had come to him. The sergeant had been at Rachel's as a potential suitor, a future husband.

He didn't want her in another man's arms. The thought set his skin crawling.

It would have been in the sergeant's best interest not to give Rachel or her father the invitation. But on the other hand, turning over the invitation to her father might just ensure Mr. Thompson pushed Rachel in the sergeant's direction. Whether he delivered it or not, the sergeant could have used the invitation to his advantage.

Lord, what do I do now? I thought inviting Rachel and her family to the party would show her father I am an honorable man. Now what?

The thought came to him again. Patience.

Hadn't he been patient enough?

He pushed his chair back with a jarring screech that made his teeth hurt. He stood and walked to the closed door and then paced from one side of his small office to the other. Back and forth. Unsettled. He had to think of something.

Glancing out the window, he saw a boy striding confidently across the grass toward a group of four marines. The men greeted the boy.

Charles turned from the window and walked across his office again. He had to figure out what to do about Rachel. But the boy kept niggling at his brain now. The way he had stridden across the lawn as though he belonged, he must be either one of the soldiers' sons or the son of one of the many English citizens on the island. But there was something familiar about the boy. When he crossed back to the window, both the boy and the knot of seamen were gone.

Charles went back to wearing a path in the floor. He jumped at the knock on the door. He rounded his desk and stood behind it. "Come in."

Private Coats opened the door. "Sir, you have a visitor."

Rachel?

"Send her in."

"It's not a her, sir. It's a boy."

A boy? "Bring him in." The boy he'd seen outside?

Coats motioned to someone beside the door.

Lindley stepped into view.

Charles almost burst with excitement but caught himself in time. He looked to Coats. "That will be all. Close the door on your way out."

Coats did as he was bid.

Once the door closed, Charles came around his desk. "Lindley, what are you doing here? You just walked straight into our camp."

The boy shrugged. "I didn't think anyone was gonna hurt me. No one wants to go to war. Not really."

"So why have you come? How is your sister? Did she get my invitation? Was your father upset? Well, say something."

"I can't with all your questions."

"I'm sorry. First, how is Rachel?"

"Fine. And no, she didn't get your invitation but Papa did, and he's really, really, really mad. He won't let Rachel leave the house."

"He's holding her a prisoner in her own home?"

"Well, not exactly a prisoner. He doesn't have her tied up or locked in her room or nothing. He said she can't leave the house, and she's obeying him. But he didn't say nothing about me staying home."

Charles wanted to smile. The boy was just like Rachel. As long as their father didn't directly tell them not to do something, they weren't directly disobeying him.

Lindley continued. "She wants to leave. Real bad."

"Is that why you came? To tell me that?"

"Naw." He reached inside his coat, pulled out two

envelopes and handed them to Charles. "She wrote this one the night you came with the invitation and this one yesterday."

Letters from Rachel. He wanted to hug them to himself as she had done with his short note he'd left with the books.

He opened the first one, three and a half pages. He quickly skimmed it. The other letter was almost two full pages. "I would like to pen a reply. Can you stay a bit?"

"Sure."

Charles opened his door. "Coats. Would you get the boy a cup of tea and some biscuits?"

Lindley scrunched up his face. "I don't want no biscuits."

He smiled at the boy. "What we call biscuits, you would call cookies."

The boy brightened. "Then I'll have two."

Charles turned back to Coats and held up four fingers. "And entertain him out here for a bit? His name is Lindley."

"Of course, sir." Coats directed Lindley away.

"Make sure the captain doesn't see him."

Coats turned back. "He left camp at dawn. Won't be back until lunch."

Charles nodded, closing his door all but two inches. He wanted some privacy but also wanted to hear if anything erupted out in the main room. He sat at his desk and unfolded the first letter.

My dearest Charles,

He read the opening salutation three times and the *my dearest* a couple more.

Then he continued with the body of the letter, which started with a quotation from *Romeo and Juliet*.

My only love sprung from my only hate!
Too early seen unknown, and known too late!
Prodigious birth of love it is to me,
That I must love a loathed enemy.

It rankled him that she used a quotation with the word *enemy* in it, but felt joy that she loved him.

She went on for the rest of the first page and all of the second about how her father was being unfair and was closed-minded. How, if he would just listen to reason, this whole romance wouldn't be a problem. On the next page she told Charles that she loved him, and if her father would meet him, he would see that Charles was a good man.

Charles liked that Rachel thought of him so highly. He never would have imagined.

The last half of a page conveyed her hope that Charles could find a way to get through to her father.

She was putting her faith in him to resolve their situation. *Lord, help me find a way.*

Then she signed it.

My heart belongs to you, my love.
Rachel

He reread her closing: *My heart belongs to you, my love.*

He may once have thought her of a silly, sentimental bent with an extra seasoning of the dramatic, but now he cherished her theatrical, romantic flare. She wasn't vacuous. She was passionate.

Her next letter also began with a quotation from *Romeo and Juliet*.

'Tis but thy name that is my enemy;
Thou art thyself, though not a Montague.
What's Montague? it is nor hand, nor foot,
Nor arm, nor face, nor any other part
Belonging to a man. O, be some other name!
What's in a name? That which we call a rose
By any other name would smell as sweet;
So Romeo would, were he not Romeo call'd,
Retain that dear perfection which he owes
Without that title. Romeo, doff thy name,
And for that name which is no part of thee
Take all myself.

If it were as easy as changing his name, Charles would in a heartbeat. But the name Thompson was English by origin. At least Thompson wasn't an O'Leary or O'Malley or other Irish name. That could make his family's acceptance of her much harder.

Rachel continued the letter about her love for him and her plight. She was growing restless in the walls of her house. She sounded a whit desperate.

Then she closed with another *Romeo and Juliet* quotation.

Two households, both alike in dignity,
In fair Verona, where we lay our scene,
From ancient grudge break to new mutiny,
Where civil blood makes civil hands unclean.
From forth the fatal loins of these two foes
A pair of star-cross'd lovers take their life;
Whose misadventured piteous overthrows
Do with their death bury their parents' strife.

When he had first met Rachel, he couldn't get her to speak until she started reciting this quotation. He had enjoyed tossing the lines back and forth with her like a game of lawn tennis. Now the quotation held so much more meaning. How similar Romeo and Juliet's plight was to his and Rachel's. Applied to real life, the quotation was dark and foreboding. This was no game.

Why did she always quote *Romeo and Juliet*? That story didn't end well. He needed to make sure their own story had a happy ending. His arms ached to enfold her safely in them. He pulled out a sheet of paper, dipped his pen in the inkwell and touched the tip to paper. He, too, began his letter with a quotation from her favorite play.

My bounty is as boundless as the sea,
My love as deep; the more I give to thee,
The more I have, for both are infinite.

He prayed that would encourage her. Help her cling to the hope of a favorable conclusion. Then he asked her to hold out hope for them. Though he didn't have a plan at the ready, he believed God had brought them together and He would give him the solution. He was of the conviction that all would work out for them.

Now that they were no longer sneaking around and he hadn't seen her in over a week, he was more convinced than ever that they would be together at some point. He hoped it would be sooner rather than later. The Lord had given him a peace about it. He wished he knew what the Almighty had planned.

Rachel simply needed to trust the Lord for their future. The Lord would hold them up and strengthen them. He left all his doubts out of the letter and just conveyed positivity and hope. Then he ended with another quotation, *Romans* 15:13:

Now may the God of hope fill you with all joy and peace in believing, that ye may abound in hope, through the power of the Holy Ghost.

Rachel ached to read Charles's letter but hadn't dared until now, well after supper. Lindley had slipped it to her when he arrived home from school. She had taken a lantern out to the barn. She sat in the loft with Mariposa and her kittens frolicking.

My dearest Rachel,
My bounty is as boundless as the sea,
My love as deep; the more I give to thee,
The more I have, for both are infinite.

She loved that quotation, in which Romeo professed the depth of his love. She had dreamed of having a man love her as Romeo had loved Juliet but knew that wasn't likely, and here she had it.

She read on.

Chapter 16

Charles rode on horseback into American Camp at the south end of the island.

One of the enlisted men approached him and took hold of the horse's halter. "Good day, sir. What can I do for you?"

Charles wasn't this soldier's superior, so the soldier needn't call him *sir*. But he appreciated the respect even from the opposition. He swung down and handed the reins to the man. The brittle winter grass crunched beneath his feet. "I've come to see..." he paused to remember the American pronunciation "...Lieutenant Bishop."

The man pointed across the compound. "He's supervising target practice."

"Thank you. Would you see that my horse gets watered?"

"Of course, sir."

Charles strode off in the direction of his newfound friend and the echo of gunfire. As he came over the rise, he saw Bishop right off, and the noncommissioned offi-

cer nearest the lieutenant saw Charles. The NCO looked
as though he could be Sergeant Hicks, whom Charles had
seen at Rachel's. He spoke to the lieutenant.

Bishop turned and waved, said something to the NCO
and headed toward Charles across the dry grass. Charles
waited where he was out of respect for his opponent's
military strategy. Spying was not the purpose of his visit
and could hamper his objective.

Bishop smiled and held out his hand. "Charles, so good
to see you."

Charles shook his friend's hand. It was strange to consider an officer in the rival's military a friend. Who could
ever have imagined? If they had been on the same side
in this war, they would have saluted one another. "I hope
those targets aren't supposed to be Englishmen."

Bishop shrugged. "They are whomever the enemy happens to be."

Charles made a show of swallowing hard and pulling
at his collar with one finger.

Bishop chuckled. "What brings you so far south, my
friend?"

"I have a little problem I'm hoping you can assist me
with."

"It depends on the problem. If you want me to hand
over the San Juan Islands to the English, I'm afraid I
don't carry the rank for that. Not that I would, even if I
had the authority."

Suddenly, Charles wasn't in a hurry for the land possession dispute to be resolved. For when it was, either he or
Rachel would be leaving the island. He doubted Rachel's
father would stay under British rule, and Charles certainly
couldn't stay if the United States was granted possession.
"Nothing so exotic. I need to speak to an American. I
think the conversation will go more smoothly if another
American is present. Preferably a military officer."

"To whom do you need to speak?"

"Warren Thompson."

Bishop let out a long whistle. "You don't ask for anything simple. It might be easier to hand over the islands."

"Then you know Mr. Thompson? You can take me to speak with him?"

"Did you not hear his first name when you said it? *War*ren. He is very patriotic. What do you need to talk to him about?"

Charles didn't want to say but knew Bishop would find out eventually when Charles spoke to Mr. Thompson. And it would be only fair to the lieutenant to let him know what he was getting himself into. "His daughter."

Bishop took a step back. "You're the one?"

"The one what?"

"Sergeant Hicks was at the Thompsons' place. He said an English officer came and delivered an invitation to your annual Christmas party. We all thought that was a bold move. Stupid, but bold. You're lucky the sergeant was there. Are you trying to ignite this war? Or get yourself shot?"

"Is the man really as bad as all that?"

"No, Mr. Thompson is a good man. He's just passionate about his belief that these islands are the territory of the United States of America, and the English don't belong here. He will try to use your visit as leverage to insist we remove the English military from the islands."

"He doesn't have the power to do that, does he?"

"No, but he will speak to Captain Pickett. And in turn, Pickett will speak to your captain."

"So this ends badly?"

"Only if Thompson talks to you at all."

"So is there no hope of him speaking with me?"

"He doesn't need to know you were the one at his home. You can just forget his daughter and let sleeping dogs lie."

"I cannot forget her. I could try, but even after a lifetime, she would still be entwined in my heart."

"Is she really worth poking a stick into a hornets' nest for?"

"Why does it have to be a hornets' nest? Why can it not be two men having a peaceful conversation?"

"Because you are English, and Thompson has devoted his life to seeing these islands officially becoming the property of the United States."

"I have to try. It'll be my funeral."

Lieutenant Bishop lowered his head. "It'll be all of ours."

"So, you'll help me."

"Tell me why it is so important that you would risk all this?"

Charles didn't know what else to say, so he spoke the simple truth. "I love her."

Bishop smiled. "There is no fool like a fool in love."

"I'm afraid I might be the court jester of fools."

"Let's hope not. Let's hope Thompson has at least one romantic bone in his patriotic body."

"Or cherishes his daughter's happiness?"

Bishop shook his head. "You have to do exactly as I say."

"I will."

"Do you know where the Belle Vue Sheep Farm is?"

"That's owned by the British Hudson's Bay Company."

"So you do know it? Meet me at the crossroads leading to it."

"Why there?"

"Thompson is the island land commissioner. He's been nagging our captain for years to allow him to do some surveying out there. Pickett has been reluctant to grant his request. And Thompson has honored that and stayed away."

"I don't believe Bazalgette would have any objections."

"That is beside the point. My commander doesn't want to owe your commander a favor."

So pride was on the line. "This will be a trade of favors."

Bishop nodded.

"I'll swing by the farm and let them know we'll be coming tomorrow."

The next day, with dark clouds approaching from the west, Charles sat upon his horse at the crossroads, awaiting the arrival of Bishop and Rachel's father, already more than half an hour late. Maybe the lieutenant couldn't persuade Mr. Thompson to come.

How much longer should he wait before this was futile? If Bishop had been completely unsuccessful, he would have come to inform him so. Charles would just have to bide his time.

He galloped his mount up the road in the direction from which he anticipated they would arrive but saw no signs of them. He headed back to the crossroads. The lieutenant and Rachel's father sat upon their own horses, waiting.

It did not look good for him to be the one who was late, though he hadn't been, but that was the way it would appear to Mr. Thompson. He stopped his horse next to Bishop's. Charles was about to explain why he was absent when they arrived, when Mr. Thompson shook his head.

It would be best to let Mr. Thompson think what he may. "Excuse my tardiness. Were you waiting long?"

"We just arrived." Bishop turned to Rachel's father. "Mr. Thompson, this is Lieutenant Young. He will be our escort today. Lieutenant, may I present Warren Thompson, land commissioner and surveyor."

Charles tipped his hat. "Pleased to meet you, sir."

"I won't lie. I'm not pleased about this meeting, but I do appreciate you getting me on the Belle Vue Farm."

He pointed in the direction of the farm. "Can we get on with this?"

Bishop nodded, and Mr. Thompson headed off down the road.

Charles took a deep breath. "Is it just my uniform or did you tell him why I'm here?"

"Full disclosure, my man. Full disclosure. Thompson is not a man it would be wise to have a hidden agenda with or spring your intentions on at the last minute." Bishop goaded his horse into motion.

Charles kicked his horse and caught up. "So he gets what he wants, and I have to hope he will keep up his end of the bargain?"

"Something like that. But Thompson is a man of his word."

"You're sure about that?"

"If he weren't, he wouldn't need our escort today. He would already have surveyed this area against Captain Pickett's edict."

This could well be a very long day with no guarantees that Charles would get what he desired out of the bargain. He would need to be patient. *Lord, grant me patience. And please let Rachel's father listen to my petition.*

Mr. Thompson stopped several times on the road heading into the farm. He pulled out his compass and other instruments and wrote figures on paper. During the course of the trip, he also took a large sheet of paper from a portfolio and sketched a map of the area.

Charles looked over his shoulder. "Very good. You depict the geological features quite accurately. I can see why you're a surveyor." He shifted his gaze from the map to Mr. Thompson's glaring face.

Couldn't the man take a compliment?

Charles stepped away. A very long day indeed.

After over four hours of trailing Mr. Thompson all

over the Belle Vue Sheep Farm and adjoining lands, they were finally heading back to the crossroads. The wind had kicked up and rain would begin soon. Still following Mr. Thompson, Charles felt like a peasant or his servant. He honestly couldn't understand this man's animosity toward him and the English. Would he even give Charles a chance to speak to him?

Charles goaded his horse to a trot and caught up with Mr. Thompson at the crossroads.

Mr. Thompson stopped and turned his horse before Charles could call out to him to stop.

"Mr. Thompson, now it is my turn."

Mr. Thompson held up his hand to quiet Charles. "Save your breath. I forbid you to seek out my daughter. Do not set foot on my land. If you do, I will shoot you as a trespasser. You have been forewarned." He lifted his reins to turn his horse.

"Mr. Thompson, I beg your pardon, but I have followed you around half a day and been very patient with the understanding that I would be granted an audience with you and be able to speak my mind. I have been respectful, and now I demand you hear me out."

"Nothing you say will sway me." But Mr. Thompson gave a nod for Charles to say his piece.

"How have I wronged you?"

"Not you personally. It's your country and what you stand for and whom you fight for. England is overbearing and takes what it likes without consideration for others."

"And what has England taken from you?"

"My home."

"Your home doesn't belong to England." It might if England was granted possession of the San Juan Islands. But that hadn't happened yet.

"Not my home here on San Juan. When the Oregon Treaty was signed, *all* of Vancouver Island was granted to

England. Even the portion south of the forty-ninth parallel. England was to have everything north but somehow managed to gain a large portion of an island clearly in United States territory."

Mr. Thompson thought that Vancouver Island should have been split between the two countries? Though Scotland was technically part of the British Isles under the governorship of England, they were always trying to become their own entity. It just didn't make sense for an island not to be part of the same country. So it had made sense that all of Vancouver Island be granted to England.

"You had a home on Vancouver?"

"It wasn't enough that I lost my first wife and my unborn son and can never visit where they or my parents are buried. I lost my home. Had to start over here. And now England wants to take that, as well."

None of that was Charles's fault. He needed to direct the conversation back to its original purpose. "About your daughter."

"There is no argument you can make to persuade me to change my mind. My daughter is off-limits. And that is final."

"Sir, I wish you would reconsider your position on me. I love your daughter."

Mr. Thompson narrowed his eyes. "You love her? You have spent enough time with *my* daughter *unchaperoned* behind *my back* to know that you love her? And you wonder what you have done to *wrong* me?"

"It all happened quite by accident." If only he had let Rachel run off after her brother that first day. But she had intrigued him, and he'd grown stultified with this uneventful war. "Nothing inappropriate has happened between Rachel and me."

Mr. Thompson raised his eyebrows.

Other than the unsupervised meeting behind his back.

"Regardless of how it happened, I love your daughter and she loves me. Do you not want her to be happy?"

"Happiness is something romantics and fools strive for. To live a contented life serving the Lord should be one's goal. God never promised us happiness on this earth. That will come in the hereafter. I have made my decision, and I expect you to abide by it."

"So you won't reconsider attending our Christmas soiree?"

"Soiree?"

"That means party."

Mr. Thompson shook his head. "Then why don't you just say so? No, I won't. Do I have your word that you will stay away from Rachel?"

How could he agree to stay away from part of himself? *Honor.*

He nodded his assent. "Keeping her away from me won't stop either one of us from loving the other. It may only serve to turn your daughter against you."

"That will be my problem. And the problem of the man I find to be her husband."

That was like a knife twisted in Charles's heart, and Mr. Thompson knew it.

Mr. Thompson turned his horse and galloped off.

Well, Charles's prayer had been answered. Mr. Thompson *had* listened. And answered with a resounding *no*! Charles should have prayed for Mr. Thompson to soften his opinion toward him. *Lord?*

Bishop moved his horse next to Charles's. "That went well."

Charles swung his gaze to the lieutenant. "Well?"

"Neither of you tried to kill the other. This war didn't get ignited into bloodshed."

"He barely listened to me. He had his mind made up before he ever came and wasn't going to change it."

"Did you really expect anything else?"

"I'd hoped."

"Be happy we don't have to report to our commanders that we got this war riled up over a girl."

"But I am no closer to Rachel than I was this morning."

"You didn't kill her pa nor he you. I'd say that is something. My best advice to you would be to forget about this girl."

"That would be like forgetting my own hand." He would need to pray for guidance.

Chapter 17

Rachel kneaded the bread dough. They would have fresh bread for supper tonight. The wind howled outside. It was going to be a long, stormy night.

At midafternoon, she heard Papa's wagon arriving in the yard. He would have the children with him. The children blew into the house on a gust of air. Genevieve gave each of them a leftover biscuit from breakfast and set out a jar of raspberry jam. Once they had eaten, she sent the two younger ones off to play in the parlor and ordered the two older ones to get busy with their schoolwork.

Papa stomped in after putting the wagon and horse away.

Genevieve went to him and helped him off with his coat. "I fear we are in for a rough night."

Papa didn't reply to her. Instead he pointed to Lindley and Alice. "Go up to your rooms and take the little ones with you."

Lindley spoke up. "But Mama said we had to get our schoolwork done before supper if we want dessert."

"Go!" Papa barked.

Alice scooped up her book and ushered Winnie and Edith up the stairs.

Lindley stared at Papa and moved deliberately slowly, closing his book, pushing away from the table, standing and finally walking to the stairs.

Something was wrong with Papa. And whatever was upsetting him had something to do with Rachel. She knew because he hadn't looked at her since he arrived home.

But she hadn't been told to stay, so she draped a towel over the bread and turned toward the stairs.

"Hold up, Rachel."

She turned to Papa's stern face. He pointed toward the parlor. She headed in that direction. He tilted his head to Genevieve to come, as well. Rachel couldn't think what she had done to upset Papa. *Oh, no. Please don't let Papa have found me a husband.*

Rachel stood by the fireplace.

Genevieve sat on the settee.

Papa pulled the pocket doors closed and turned with a disapproving glance to her.

"Papa, I promise I haven't left the house. You can ask Genevieve."

Papa held up a hand to silence her. "Sit."

She would rather stand but moved to the nearest chair and lowered herself into it.

Papa paced behind her. Genevieve's gaze darted between Rachel and Papa. Her stepmother gave nothing away, if she even knew anything. Papa came around the chairs and stared at Rachel, his hands clasped behind his back.

She wished Papa would say something. Give her some clue as to what this was about.

He opened his mouth to speak, but a shutter banging

against the house stopped him. "Don't move." He strode outside to batten down the shutter.

Once Papa was out of the room, Rachel pinned Genevieve with her gaze. "What is Papa upset about?"

"He hasn't told me yet. I guess I'll find out when you do."

"You don't think he found a husband for me and is going to force me to marry someone I don't want to, do you?"

"Your father's not cruel. I don't believe he would make you marry someone you are opposed to. He truly wants the best for you."

"I know who would be best for me."

Genevieve narrowed her eyes. "You would be wise not to mention him or the English."

"Why does Papa hate them so?"

The door opened, and Papa came back inside.

Genevieve lowered her voice. "It's not your place to question. That you know he hates them should be enough." She turned as Papa entered and smiled up at him. "Is the shutter secure?"

He slid the pocket doors closed again. "Yes. I checked the rest around the house. That one always gives us trouble." Papa went back to pacing behind Rachel's chair. He evidently needed to collect his thoughts again. Fortunately, it didn't take as long this time. He had calmed down even more since he first came home. Battening down the shutter seemed to have been a good thing.

He stood in front of Rachel once again. "A particular lieutenant came to speak to me today about you."

Another suitor? First a sergeant, now a lieutenant. If Papa was so against the English, she wished he would just let her grow into an old maid. She would be happier living under Papa's roof until she was old than with a man she didn't love. But she knew it was best to keep her comments to herself and let Papa say all he was going to.

"Don't worry. I told him to stay away from you and not to set foot on our property."

A bad feeling pinched Rachel's insides, and she could feel the blood drain from her face.

"Yes. Lieutenant Young of the English military paid me a visit. I have forbidden him to see you. And if he steps onto my property, I will shoot him as a trespasser. So you can forget all about him. You will never see him again."

"But, Papa—"

"This is not a discussion."

"Please, at least get to know him. He is a fine man."

Papa's voice rose. "A fine man! He's English! I will not allow any daughter of mine to go cavorting around with the enemy. He said he loves you. Just how long have you been sneaking off to see him?"

She didn't want to answer that but knew she must. "A couple of months." That was fudging the truth. It was more than three months. But two months, four month or a year would all be just as bad to Papa. "Nothing happened between us. I promise. He was a perfect gentleman."

"Nothing happened! Perfect gentleman! He is no kind of gentleman. A gentleman wouldn't have been sneaking around with another man's daughter. He would have come to me first. And as far as nothing happening, the man claims to be in love with you. That is not nothing. That is a man with clandestine intentions."

"No, Papa. It wasn't like that. It just happened."

"He said the same thing. Two people don't just happen to keep meeting repeatedly. You know how I feel about the English. You should never have been anywhere near the English. If you saw an English person, especially a man, you should have run in the other direction."

"Won't you at least consider meeting him?"

"I've met him. You are not to see him or seek him out ever again."

"Can't you try to like him?"

"No."

"But you don't know anything about him."

"All I need to know is that he's English."

Rachel stood. "That's not fair!"

"Fair or not, that is the way it is. And you *will* abide by my wishes."

"Please, Papa. I'm begging you to give him a chance. I'm sure you'll like him."

"I'm sure I won't."

"But I love him." She knew she shouldn't have said that as soon as the words crossed her lips.

"You are never seeing him again. Never!"

Both pocket doors to the parlor pushed open quickly and banged inside the walls. Lindley stood in the doorway. "That's not fair!"

Papa glared. "Lindley, go to your room. This doesn't concern you."

Her half brother stepped into the room. "Leftenant Young is a good man. He's nice."

Papa strode over to Lindley. "What do you know of this Lieutenant Young?"

Rachel spoke up. "Lindy, don't. You can't help."

Papa held up a hand to her. "I want to hear what my son knows. Lindley? You've met Lieutenant Young?"

Lindley squared his shoulders. "Yes, I have. He's teaching me to sword fight."

"Have you seen him on more than one occasion?"

"Lots and lots of times."

Rachel wished her brother would stop. He wasn't helping her and was only getting himself into trouble now.

Papa turned to her. "Did you take him?"

She was about to say yes to lessen Lindley's likely punishment, but her brother spoke more quickly.

"I followed Rachel at first." Lindley was talking in as loud a voice as Papa. "Then I went myself. The English are not bad. Leftenant Young is a nice man. And you are being unfair to Rachel."

"That's enough from you, young man. Go to your room, and I'll deal with you later."

"No, I won't." Lindley whirled around.

Rachel had never heard her brother talk to their father in such a fashion. The front door slammed open. Lindley continued his protest by stomping across the porch.

Papa went after him to the door. "Lindley! Get back here!"

"No!" her brother called back.

She could tell by the warble in his voice that he was running.

The door closed, and Papa returned to the parlor.

Genevieve stood up. "Aren't you going after him?"

"He ran out to the barn. He'll be back when he gets hungry." Papa turned on Rachel. "See where your defiance has taken this family? You have caused your brother to disobey, as well. The younger ones look up to you as the oldest. You have a responsibility to set a good example."

She was not the one who caused Lindley to disobey. It was Papa's unyieldingness, his unwillingness to listen. "May I go to my room?"

Papa gave her a nod. "But be back down in an hour to help with supper."

Tears burned Rachel's eyes as she ran up the stairs. Papa was being so unfair. Why wouldn't he at least listen? She opened the door to her room, and three pairs of her sisters' eyes stared up at her. She grabbed *Romeo and Juliet* off the dresser and stepped back into the hall, closing the door behind her. She didn't want to have to explain to them why she was upset or even look at them. She wanted to be alone. Normally, she would head out into the woods, but she was forbidden, so she went into Lindley's room and closed the door. He wouldn't mind. She sat on his bed and opened the book to the pressed flower. The fragrance had left it. Unfolding the letter from Charles next, she reread it.

She covered her face and let the tears fall. Maybe she would run away. Charles had once teased that they could get married in secret like Romeo and Juliet and run off together. She wished she'd taken him up on his offer.

But that would start the war going. Papa would make sure of it. He would probably accuse Charles of kidnapping her.

Lord, please change Papa's mind. Show him that Charles is a good man. I love him.

Three hours later, as Rachel was helping Genevieve put the last of the food on the table, she turned to Papa. "I'm not hungry. May I go to my room?" She didn't want to sit at the table with Papa or any of them. She wanted to be alone. And while preparing supper, she had snuck bites of food so she wouldn't be hungry.

Papa studied her for a moment. "Very well. But go get your brother. He's been out there long enough."

Gladly. She was allowed outside only to use the privy, so this was a welcome treat.

"Put on your coat," Genevieve said. "The rain is coming down."

Though Rachel was an adult, Genevieve still tried to mother her. Rachel didn't mind the rain. It made everything smell fresh and clean. But she put on her coat. It would be good against the cold that came with the rain. She tugged Lindley's coat off the wall hook, as well. He was probably quite cold from being out there all this time.

Papa handed her a lantern as she went out.

She ducked her face against the blowing rain. The cold, wet air slipped into her lungs. At the barn, she pulled the door open only far enough to squeeze inside the dark interior. Her poor brother out here without light and in the cold. "Lindy?"

She listened, but no reply came. So she called more loudly, "Lindy, where are you? It's just me, Rachel."

She searched the stalls. "Supper's ready."

He must be in the loft. Probably fell asleep. With the lantern in one hand, she climbed the ladder. Lindley was nowhere in sight. She maneuvered over to where she'd last seen Mariposa and her kittens. And there they were. The kittens were all piled on top of each other, sleeping.

She bent down and petted the mama. "Where's Lindy? Do you know?"

The cat leaned into her hand.

Rachel trudged around the loft until she was sure Lindley wasn't up there. She called out again. "Lindy! Where are you?"

She climbed down from the loft and searched the lower portion of the barn again. Other than the livestock, there wasn't anyone there.

She left the barn and went out to the privy. He wasn't there either. She looked around the yard as she headed back to the house. "Lindy! Lindy!"

When she stepped inside, everyone was at the table waiting, and Papa asked, "What took so long?"

"Lindy's gone. I can't find him anywhere."

Papa stood, grabbed his coat and took the lantern from her before heading out the door.

Genevieve came over to her. "I know you looked everywhere. Where could he be?"

"I don't know."

After a few minutes, Papa came back in. "He's gone. I'm going to get a few men and go looking for him."

Genevieve clasped her hands to her chest.

Rachel wrapped a supportive arm around her.

Papa kissed Genevieve. "I'll find him and bring him home." He left.

Genevieve shooed Rachel to the table. "Everyone eat."

Rachel sat as Genevieve bid. But no one reached for any of the food.

Genevieve looked around the table at the girls. "Well. Eat."

Alice began to cry. "But we haven't said grace."

Rachel took her littlest sisters' hands on either side of her. Genevieve and Alice completed the circle. Rachel prayed for safe travel for Papa and for him to find Lindley safe and sound. After the blessing, Rachel dished food onto Winnie's and Edith's plates as well as her own. Genevieve and Alice put food on their own plates. But no one ate. They just stared at their food.

Finally, Genevieve spoke. "Where could my baby boy have gone?"

"I don't know." Rachel pictured her brother laughing, playing, running through the woods. Then she pictured him sword fighting with Charles. Charles was so good with Lindley. If Papa hadn't been so stubborn about Charles, Lindley wouldn't have run off.

Rachel ceased breathing. Neither in nor out. Lindley wouldn't have. Would he?

He would.

Exhaling, she pushed away from the table.

"Where are you going?" Genevieve asked.

Rachel shrugged on her coat. "I think I know where Lindy could have gone."

Genevieve gripped her arm. "You can't go out in this weather."

Rachel took her stepmother's hand from her arm and

held it. "Lindy is out in this. I have to try. I know the woods well. I'll be fine."

Genevieve's hand tightened. "Your father would never forgive me if I let you go out and something happened to you."

"He'll never forgive himself if something happens to his only son. I have to go. You can't stop me."

Genevieve studied Rachel's face for several moments. "You think he's at their camp, don't you?"

She nodded.

"Bring him home."

"I will. And if Papa asks me, I'll tell him you did everything in your power to stop me."

Genevieve put a gentle hand on Rachel's cheek. "You have always been a good daughter." She put a brimmed hat on Rachel's head and tied a scarf around it to keep it in place. "God's speed. I'll pray until all my family is safely home."

Rachel kissed her stepmother's cheek. "Thank you." She lit the spare lantern and stepped outside.

Lord, let me find him. Please let him be safe.

The wind lashed rain against her face. She pushed forward, across the yard and into the woods. The fir tree canopy acted as an umbrella, shielding her from the rainfall. The few drops that did make it to the forest floor were large accumulations, more like being doused with cups of water than individual raindrops. The thick growth of trees and underbrush broke the force of the wind and made travel manageable. Even though Rachel knew her way, she still found it difficult in the dark with the storm. If this had been a clear night, a full moon would have lit her way. As it was, the ground was soggy, the undergrowth dripping and the going slow with mud sucking at her boots.

Please, Lord, please let Lindy be safe.

Chapter 18

Charles sat near the potbelly stove in the dining hall where the men were gathered. Wind lashed rain against the windows and pushed cold air in through invisible cracks. He held his hands around his cup of tea. It was almost cool enough to drink without scalding his tongue.

He went over the events of the day. Could he have done something different to have swayed Mr. Thompson in his favor? Mr. Thompson had said there wasn't anything he could say to change his mind.

The outside door opened, and the din of the men inside silenced immediately, so he looked up to see who had come in. Probably Captain Bazalgette. He couldn't imagine anyone else commanding their attention so quickly and making them all stand. But when he saw who it was, Charles abandoned his tea and rushed over.

Rachel?

She looked cold, and rain dripped off her. Her skirt, her coat and even her face were splattered with mud.

He took her elbow and ushered her over to the stove. "What are you doing out in this storm? What are you doing here at camp?" He pulled off her mittens and rubbed her cold hands between his.

"Is he here?" she asked in a thin, tired voice.

"Who?" Her father?

"Lindley." Her voice gained strength. "He ran away. Is he here?"

"No, I haven't seen him." He grabbed his cup of tea from the nearby table. "Here. Drink this. It will help warm you."

She cradled it in her hands and drank it down.

"Why would he run away?"

"I had a big fight with Papa. Lindy stood up for me… and you. We all thought he was just out in the barn sulking."

"Was the fight about my visit with your father earlier today?"

She nodded.

"What is she doing here?" thundered the captain's voice.

The men turned, straightened and shuffled backward to make a path for their superior.

Charles stood at attention. "Sir, Miss Thompson came looking for her brother. He's out in this storm, and she thought he might have wandered into camp."

His captain's stern face softened slightly. "How old is he?"

Rachel stood. "Only twelve. I meant no harm in coming."

He turned. "Sergeant, organize the men into search parties."

The men scattered to get their gear on to brave the weather. Not one of them complained about going out in a storm to search for an American boy.

Rachel spoke to the captain. "You don't have to do that."

Captain Bazalgette gazed down at her. "I would be remiss as a gentleman, not to mention as a human being, if we didn't aid in the search."

"Thank you."

He nodded. "You'd best head on back home before they come looking for you, as well."

Charles spoke up then. "I'll see she makes it back home safely."

Rachel opened her mouth to speak, but Charles gripped her arm to silence her.

Captain Bazalgette studied him a moment. "Very well. Then join up with one of the search parties."

"Yes, sir."

The captain walked away.

Charles helped Rachel back into the chair. "You stay here and warm yourself by the stove. I'll get what I need and be right back."

Rachel grabbed his arm this time. "I'm not going home. I'm going to look for my brother."

He patted her hand. "I know."

"Then why did you tell your commander you would take me home?"

"He would not have accepted you, a lady, continuing in the search. And after we find Lindley, I *will* see you safely home."

She seemed pleased with his answer and released his arm. He missed her touch but went to dress for the storm. He donned his rain gear. The men scurried around in preparation to head out. He stopped by the table where a map had been spread out and told the sergeant the direction he would be heading in with Rachel. Then he returned to her. "Are you warming up?"

"Yes, I feel much better. Let's go." She reached for her coat, which hung on the back of a chair.

He stopped her and held up two raincoats. "Your coat is soaked through. Put these on." He set one down and held up the smaller of the two.

She poked her arms into the sleeves. "I don't think I need two. One will suffice."

He fastened the coat on her. "The second is for Lindley. He will likely be wet and cold. It will be easier if you wear the second rather than trying to carry it. When we find your brother, the coat will already be warmed for him." And it would keep her warmer as well until then.

She grabbed the cuffs of the coat she had on and held them in her fists as she pushed her arms into the second set of sleeves. The coats hung big on her and nearly touched the ground. She would be well protected. He gave her a dry hat and hoped she would be warm enough. The search could take a while.

Lord, please help us to find him and bring him back safely.

As they were heading for the door, Charles noticed a coil of rope on the floor. His men knew better than to leave something like that lying around.

For some reason he couldn't explain, he felt he should take it.

Without thinking about it more, he scooped up the rope and hiked it over his shoulder.

"What's that for?" Rachel asked.

"I'm not sure. I just get the impression I should bring it." He took the lantern from her.

She didn't question him further and scurried out the door. "Which direction?"

The wind and rain accosted him before he could even close the door behind them. He pointed toward the hill she had come down. "It must look as though I'm escorting you home. And if Lindley was indeed coming here, the woods between here and your house are the most likely place to find him."

She headed up the hill. Once at the top, she pointed. "The path is this way."

He gripped her arm. "This way. The first time I came to your house, I went the wrong way around a bush and got turned around a bit. In the dark, Lindley might have, too." He took her hand and led her along the cliff overlooking the water beyond the officers' housing.

"Lindley!"

"Lindy!"

He hoped Lindley hadn't gotten this close to the cliff, but he felt led to go this way. The guiding comforted him, assuring him that he was headed the right direction, but it also frightened him. If the boy went over the cliff, it would be bad. "The edge is close here. Stay near the trees on that side." He maneuvered Rachel over by the trees, away from the cliff, while holding the lantern up. "Lindley!"

"Lindy!"

Charles stopped short. "Dear God, no."

"What is it?"

Charles held the lamp higher as he studied the ground near the edge. The ground cover was disturbed. The floor debris had been scraped down to the dirt in places. And the marks went over the edge. *Please let it have been an animal.* He pointed. "Stay back. I'll check it out."

He inched toward the edge but couldn't get close enough to see over. He moved back, set down the lantern and then tied the rope around himself. He held the other end, using it to keep himself from slipping over the edge. He took the lantern and inched himself to the edge so he could see down the side.

"Do you see anything?"

"I can't tell." Then he saw Lindley about ten feet down. The boy clung facedown to a tree and bush growing out of the side of the cliff. He wasn't moving. "He's here." He called back to Rachel. "Stay back, though." He called down to the boy. "Lindley, can you hear me?"

The boy's reply was but a whimper.

Charles breathed more easily. He was alive. "Hold on tight. I'm coming to get you." Lindley was probably too scared and cold to move.

Charles scrambled away from the edge. Rachel stared at him. "He's down there. I heard him make a noise. I think he's just scared and cold."

She leaned around him, but he held on to her to make sure she didn't go near the muddy edge. "Lindy, we're coming for you."

Charles retied the rope around himself to rappel down the cliff better and wound the other end once around the trunk of a sturdy tree. He showed Rachel how to use the rope around the tree to increase her strength to lower him down to Lindley.

"I don't think I can do that. I'm not very strong."

Charles touched her shoulders. Rain dripped off her hat. "You can do this. Don't doubt yourself. Don't wonder if you can. Just know that you have to. You have no choice."

"What if you fall? I should be the one to go down. You're stronger."

"It's too dangerous." He would never risk her life like that. "Your skirts would be cumbersome and get in the way. You can do this." He stared into her eyes until she believed him.

She nodded.

Many a capable soldier doubted himself and failed, while other, lesser soldiers believed they could do something and succeeded. "I trust you."

With the rope behind her, she gripped it on each side of herself and planted her feet.

Charles took the lantern and inched toward the edge. He put his weight into the rope so Rachel could feel the pull and be prepared when all his weight was in her hands. *Lord, give her the strength and confidence to do this. People have been known to show considerable strength beyond their abilities in situations like this.*

Before he reached the edge, he leaned his weight on the rope. Rachel held him. He hung the lantern on a branch over the cliff so he would have a little light. And he would have both hands free to grip roots and rocks on the way down. "All right. I'm going over now."

"I'm ready."

He hoped she was. "I'm coming down to you, Lindley." As he inched closer, he slipped in the mud. He slid over the edge and dangled. His heart jumped up into his throat. He heard Rachel grunt, but she held him. He grabbed the muddy cliff and jammed the toes of his boots into the soft side. That had been scary. Lindley must have been terrified when he went over. Charles caught his breath before working his way down with Rachel releasing the rope a few inches at a time.

Though he couldn't see the water below in the inky blackness, he could hear it crashing against the base of the cliff. And there were probably large and small rocks that he would dash against if he fell. He made his way over the roots of the tree.

As he neared Lindley, he reached one leg out to stand on the tree trunk on the far side of the boy. He put his other foot through the roots coming out of the wall. The tree was solidly planted in the side of the cliff. "Hold up! I'm down!"

"All right! How is Lindy?"

"Lindley, can you hear me?"

His voice was small. "Yes." He was still facedown.

"Can you move at all?"

"I'm afraid to. I don't want to fall more."

"Do you think you are hurt badly?"

"I don't think so. I'm really cold." Lindley's teeth chattered.

Charles called up to Rachel. "He's fine! Just cold!" He hoped that was all that was wrong. He leaned forward to grab hold of Lindley before the boy moved. The rope kept Charles from reaching him. "Give me about six inches!"

The rope slackened.

He looped one arm through a thick root and gripped the waist of the boy's trousers with his free hand. "I want you to stand up and hold on to me."

Lindley moved, and his hand slipped off the trunk. "Aaah!"

"It's all right. I've got you."

Lindley worked his way onto his knees, then caught Charles's leg and pulled himself up. He quickly hooked his arms around Charles's waist.

To give Lindley enough room to stand balanced, Charles leaned back slightly, holding himself up by the arm he had looped through the root. His other arm was securely around the boy. He untied the rope with one hand. He pushed his arm farther through the root so he could use both hands to tie the rope around Lindley.

The boy was secure, but Charles's stomach knotted as he felt his foot slip off the trunk. His leg swung out over thin air. If not for his arm around the root, he would have plunged to his death.

Lindley cried out.

"I'm all right." He pulled himself back up onto the

trunk behind the boy and then took a moment to catch his breath. He called up to Rachel. "Start pulling!"

He told Lindley, "Climb the roots as far as you can. Then dig your hands and feet into the muddy side."

Lindley nodded. Up the boy went, over the roots.

Charles pushed from below to help both the boy and Rachel. Once Lindley got to the top of the roots, he didn't ascend any higher.

"Pull, Rachel!"

"I am!"

She wasn't strong enough. It was one thing to lower a person but quite another to pull someone up. If she couldn't pull the boy up, did Lindley have a chance? *Lord, give her the strength.*

Then the boy started rising.

Charles breathed a sigh of relief. She had found the strength.

The shadow of the boy slipped over the edge and out of sight. He waited for her to throw the rope back down to him. He waited.

And waited.

Was she having trouble untying it? "Rachel?"

A person appeared over the edge of the cliff. The light from the lantern illuminated the face.

Mr. Thompson.

That was why she'd suddenly been able to pull her brother up.

Charles's life was in the hands of a man who didn't want his daughter near him. A man who had threatened him. A man who would prefer he disappeared. Permanently.

Both men knew the power Mr. Thompson had at that moment.

Charles resisted the urge to beg for his life. *Lord, please let him make the right decision.*

Mr. Thompson disappeared.

Charles closed his eyes. *Lord, don't let him leave me down here.* Being responsible for the death of another was not something he wished for the man. And Rachel would look at her father differently for the rest of her life.

The rope hit his arm. He opened his eyes and grabbed it. He quickly tied it around himself before the man changed his mind. Would he help pull him up? Or had he felt he'd done his duty by simply throwing the rope down?

"Ready?"

Charles looked up to see Mr. Thompson. "Yes, sir."

Mr. Thompson disappeared, and the rope tightened.

Charles scrambled over the roots and climbed his way up the cliff. Near the top, he lost his footing and slipped, dangling at the mercy of his benefactor. Regaining his grip, he finished clawing his way up and over the edge. He rolled onto his back, grateful he wasn't going to have to spend the night over a cliff in the rain and wind. The rope pressed into his back. Mr. Thompson also sat back from the exertion.

Rachel looked at him but rushed to her father. "Are you all right, Papa?"

Had the man been hurt?

Mr. Thompson pushed himself up. "I'm fine."

Charles said, "Thank you, sir, for pulling me up."

Mr. Thompson stared at Charles a moment and then said to Rachel, "We need to get your brother home."

Charles quickly freed himself from the rope. "Our camp is closer. We should take him there. We have a doctor who can see to his needs."

Mr. Thompson seemed to weigh his options.

"We need to get him warm as soon as possible, sir." Charles hoped the man wasn't too proud to see reason.

Rachel helped Lindley to his feet. She had put the extra coat on him. "Please, Papa."

Lindley's legs buckled, unable to hold him up.

Mr. Thompson put his arm around his son and reached his other under the boy's legs to carry him. But he couldn't get the boy off the ground. He winced.

Rachel said, "Papa hurt his arm."

"I'm fine." The older man grimaced.

Charles put his arms out to carry the boy. "Please, sir. Let me."

Mr. Thompson nodded.

Charles scooped Lindley up. "Will you let me take him to our camp for treatment?"

He nodded again.

Charles didn't hesitate and hurried for camp, with Rachel and Mr. Thompson following. He slid most of the way down the muddy hill into camp and rushed across the parade ground to the infirmary.

The doctor greeted them. "What happened?"

"He fell over a cliff and landed on an outgrowing tree. He was there for a while, so he's cold."

"Put him on the bed closest to the stove."

Charles did and shucked off his own coat, letting it fall to the floor.

"Help me get him out of these wet clothes," the doctor ordered him.

Charles and the medical assistant made short work of the job. Lindley's skin was so cold. The assistant covered the boy with a warm blanket. The doctor quickly determined that Lindley didn't have any broken bones and was just scraped up, bruised and cold. Now the important thing was to get him warm.

Rachel took one of Lindley's muddy hands and rubbed it between hers to warm it. Mr. Thompson did the same with the other. Charles unbuttoned the middle of his shirt and tucked one of Lindley's feet on the warmth of his stomach. He gasped, startled at the temperature difference. He rubbed heat into the calf. The assistant did the same with the other foot. He seemed more prepared for the cold foot on his skin.

Charles gazed at Rachel, and she looked back at him. He wanted to go to her and hold her. He wanted to talk with her, but knew he must restrain himself with Mr. Thompson present.

The doctor peered at Charles. "Is that just mud on your face, or do I need to examine you, too?"

"Just mud." He must look a sight. "But Mr. Thompson hurt his arm."

Mr. Thompson shook his head. "I'm fine."

"No, you're not," Rachel said.

The doctor glared. "I'll be the judge of your wellness."

Soon, the doctor had Mr. Thompson's arm in a sling for a sprained shoulder. Probably from when Charles had slipped climbing up.

Captain Bazalgette came in and spoke to the doctor in hushed tones. Satisfied, he left again. Charles heard three gunshots in succession, the signal to end the search so the men would return.

The doctor came over and spoke to Mr. Thompson. "The commander is sending someone to your home to inform the rest of your family that the boy has been found and that you all are safe."

"Thank you," Mr. Thompson said.

Soon Lindley's eyes opened. "I'm hungry."

Rachel giggled and kissed her brother's forehead.

Charles could hear audible sighs from everyone in the room.

The assistant winked. "I'll see what I can rustle up."

The doctor talked Mr. Thompson into staying the night for his son's sake. Rachel and her father slept in the infirmary with Lindley. Charles knew that accepting medical help for his son and staying at the camp were hard for the man, considering how he felt about the English. He was a proud man, but not so proud that he would risk his son's life.

Chapter 19

The rain had stopped during the night, but the morning dawned to a thick fog that hugged the ground. Mr. Thompson could not be persuaded to wait until the fog burned off. So Charles hitched a wagon and put several blankets in the back. Rachel came out of the infirmary with her father and brother.

Charles hadn't gotten a moment to talk to her alone since finding her brother dangling below the cliff. He figured that by keeping his distance, he was honoring Mr. Thompson's edict to stay away from his daughter. He had missed her, and his heart ached that he had to part from her without spending any time with her. If only he could convince Mr. Thompson to give him a chance.

Charles jumped down from the wagon. "Let me help with Lindley."

Mr. Thompson narrowed his eyes. "I've got him." The man would have walked home if his son had the strength. Charles suspected that Lindley had the strength but didn't want to walk. The boy had recovered quickly.

Rachel gave Charles a sympathetic, wan smile.

Charles would try again. "Would you like to ride up on the seat with me, sir?"

"Thank you, but I'll sit in the back with my *children*." His words were direct to let Charles know he needn't bother asking Rachel to sit with him. At least he'd said thank you.

Once everyone was aboard, Charles snapped the reins, and the wagon lunged forward. This was going to be a long trip with Mr. Thompson glaring daggers at his back. Well, Charles assumed the man would be glaring at him. But the ride would probably be just as uncomfortable for Mr. Thompson.

Charles drove up to the house and halted the horse. He jumped down to help Rachel and her family out of the back, but they already had Lindley almost on his feet.

The front door flew open, and a woman in her late thirties came out and wrapped her motherly arms around her son. She looked directly at Charles. "Thank you."

Mr. Thompson spoke up. "Mama, you and Rachel take Lindley inside." They did as he bid.

Once Mr. Thompson's family was inside and the door closed, the older man turned to Charles. Then he shoved his hand out, holding it suspended in the gap between them.

Surprised, Charles stared at the offer a moment before he reached out and took the man's hand.

Mr. Thompson gave him a firm handshake. "Thank you for saving my son. My only son. If you and Rachel hadn't found him, he would have died."

Charles recalled Lindley naming off his siblings. All girls. The poor man had only one son. And that son's life had been in danger. Charles's parents had the proverbial heir and a spare with two more spares to boot. Mr. Thompson had no spares. "I was glad to be of assistance. Your son is a fine boy." He expected Mr. Thompson to take his leave, but he stayed in place.

Mr. Thompson cleared his throat. "If that invitation to the Christmas *soiree* still stands, my family would be honored to come."

Charles realized he blinked several times. He was trying to make sense of what the man had said. Had he really accepted the invitation? Or was that just what Charles had wanted him to say? "Sir?"

Mr. Thompson pulled his eyebrows together. "Are you really going to make me say it again?"

"I just can't believe you're accepting my invitation."

"Well, I am. But if you don't want us—"

"No. I definitely want you there. All of you. I just never thought you would change your mind. Not after yesterday morning."

"I'm indebted to you. I owe you my son's life."

"You owe me nothing. I was happy to aid in the search. Yes, the invitation still stands. I would be honored to have you as my guests." Feeling bolstered, he asked, "May I speak with Rachel?"

Mr. Thompson shook his head. "You'll see her in two days' time. Good day, Lieutenant."

He would see Rachel in two days' time *with* her father's approval. He was more than pleased with that. Out of respect, Charles came to attention and saluted Mr. Thompson.

Rachel did her best to peer out the window. But Genevieve wouldn't let her get too close to the window and the curtain blocked part of her view.

She saw Charles climb onto the wagon and drive away. She sighed. She'd hoped Papa would let her talk with

Charles a little. Papa had been quite civil during the whole ordeal last night. She knew it had been hard for him to accept help from the English, but he'd done so with remarkable decorum. She stepped back as Papa came inside.

Papa closed the door and hung up his coat. He wouldn't look at her. "Where is Mama?"

"She wanted to put Lindy to bed, but he fussed, so she put him in the parlor near the fire."

He went into the other room, leaving her behind.

Dared she follow? Was she welcome? Or would she be shooed away?

Papa stood at the fireplace and turned his gaze on her. "Rachel, this concerns you."

Her stomach tightened. Papa did not sound happy. With a deep breath, she strolled into the room, putting on a pleasant expression.

Alice sat in a chair with baby Priscilla on her lap. Winnie and Edith sat on the floor with their rag dolls.

Well, it couldn't be anything bad if all the little ones were present.

Papa studied her for several moments.

It made her nervous.

Finally, he spoke. "As much as it pains me, I must give credit where credit is due. If not for Lieutenant Young risking his life, I believe Lindley wouldn't have been found until morning, and I fear that would have been too late."

Rachel bubbled inside. She would in no way have wished for her brother's turmoil of the night before, but she was glad something good had come of it. *All things work together for good...*

Papa went on. "I think—against my better judgment—I have, on behalf of the whole family, accepted the lieutenant's invitation to the English Christmas Eve soiree."

Rachel stared at Papa. She knew what she thought she'd

heard, what she wanted to hear, but what had Papa actually said?

"Yippee!" Lindley said.

Papa gazed directly at her. "Well, daughter? I thought you would be happy."

Genevieve touched Papa's arm. "My dear, I do believe you have rendered your daughter speechless. I hadn't thought that possible."

Rachel found her voice. "Did you say that we will be going to the *English* Christmas party?"

"I believe they are calling it a *soiree.* But yes."

Rachel flew across the room and hugged Papa. "Thank you, Papa, thank you!" She felt his chuckle rumble in his chest.

Genevieve gasped. "That's only two days away." She stood. "We have a lot to do. Come, Rachel."

What was her stepmother up to? She followed Genevieve upstairs to the room her stepmother shared with Papa.

Genevieve knelt before an old trunk in front of the window and creaked open the lid. Then she set about pulling out several pieces of folded clothing and fabric, even a quilt, and putting them aside. She lifted out a pile of green velvet and set it on the bed. "This was mine when I was younger. I dare say I will never fit into it again, not after five children." She unfolded the skirt and matching shirtwaist. "It doesn't have any lace or fancy trim, but the fabric is good. I think we can turn it into an appropriate gown for the party."

Rachel gaped. "Oh, Genevieve, it will make a lovely gown. I've never had anything so fine. Are you sure? Don't you want to save it for Alice?"

"If we make our seams wide and keep all the leftovers, we should be able to redesign it for her, as well. You need to have a pretty dress to ensure your lieutenant knows you are the most beautiful lady there." Genevieve held the shirtwaist up to Rachel. "I think if we modify the sleeves and the neckline and adjust the fit and hem, that should be manageable."

Rachel pressed her hands to the garment and twirled around. "It will be lovely." She hugged Genevieve. "Thank you ever so much. I'll feel like Cinderella."

"Well, I have no glass slippers for you. If you are Cinderella, that makes me your cruel stepmother."

"Certainly not. You are my fairy godmother."

Charles saw Brantley outside the stable after he handed over the horse and wagon to the stable hand. "She's coming!"

"You sound like a giddy schoolgirl."

He was giddy. Rachel's father had actually accepted the invitation. No more sneaking around. "Don't you mean school*boy*?"

Brantley shook his head. "No. You are acting like a school*girl*."

Charles took the barb. He didn't care. He was happy. His prayer had been answered. He was going to see Rachel with her father's blessing. And he would do what he could to convince the older man that he'd make Rachel a good husband.

"You may have added another plank in bridging the gap between the two sides."

Charles hoped so. In more ways than one.

Chapter 20

Charles glanced out the window again. "Where are they?"

Brantley took his arm and pulled him across the room. "Gaping out the window won't hasten the lady Thompson's arrival."

The hall was decorated with red bows. The aromas of cinnamon and apple cider drifted in the air.

"You don't think Mr. Thompson changed his mind, do you? That he was just placating me when he said his family could attend?"

"The man has a passel of women who need to prepare themselves. I have only one, and we are never on time for anything. Are you sure you want the inconvenience of a wife?"

"Rachel could never be an inconvenience."

"We'll see."

His breath caught at the sight of her. His Juliet. He enjoyed the vision of her while she searched the room for him.

When her gaze came around and landed on him, her face brightened.

"This is what you've been waiting for." Brantley shoved him from behind. "Go to her."

Charles strode across the room and stopped in front of her. Taking her hand, he bowed over it. "A pleasure, milady." He was delighted to see the slight blush in her cheeks.

"You've met my papa, Warren Thompson."

Charles shook the man's hand, pleased with the firm grip he gave him. "Sir. I am happy you and your family could join us." He knew he didn't have to call the man *sir* but did so out of respect.

"Thank you for the invitation."

Rachel continued with the introductions. "This is Genevieve and baby Priscilla."

Charles bowed over Rachel's stepmother's hand and caressed the baby's cheek. "Thank you for coming."

Genevieve smiled. "You certainly have put up the decorations."

"The Lord's birth is worth celebrating." Fir boughs hung over each of the windows and adorned the refreshment table. A large decorated pine tree stood in the corner.

"My sister Alice," Rachel said.

Charles took Alice's hand and bowed. "Milady."

Alice giggled, and her face reddened.

He was introduced to Winnie and Edith and, of course, Lindley, who had recovered well from his peril three days prior.

Captain Bazalgette came over, and Charles introduced him to Rachel's family.

The captain gave a nod. "I'm pleased you and your family could attend our little gathering."

Charles offered his elbow to Rachel. "Would you care for some apple cider?"

After glancing at her father for approval, she looped her hand through his arm.

He guided her to the refreshment table and handed her a cup of cider. All this formality felt stiff. He'd always had a relaxed relationship with Rachel. But he mustn't make even one misstep if he was to gain Mr. Thompson's trust. And eventually his daughter.

Charles gave a deep bow. "May I have this dance?"

"I don't know any fancy dances."

"This is a waltz. It has a three-count tempo. One, two, three. One, two, three." He set her cup on the table and held out his hand to her. "May I have the honor of instructing you?" It would give him an acceptable excuse to hold her in his arms.

"You think you can teach a simple island girl?"

"Miss Thompson, there is nothing simple about you."

She fitted her hand in his, and he led her to the edge of the other dancing pairs.

He placed her left hand on his right shoulder and then took her right hand in his left while hooking his other arm around her waist. He held her more than the prescribed distance away from himself so that her father might not object. Though tempted, he refused to look at the man in case he wore a disapproving glare.

"See how we form a box with our bodies?"

Rachel glanced from their arms on one side to the ones on the other and nodded.

"Now keep your carriage straight." He pushed on her right hand, and her elbow bent. "Keep your elbow stiff so that when I move, you move with me."

"I can do that."

"You will start with your right foot. Take a step back." He took a step forward at the same time. He was pleased that she remembered to keep her body stiff. "That was one. Now your left foot goes back and out. Two. Bring your right foot next to your left. Three. We are going to do the same thing except I will go back and you will move forward for a three count." He counted aloud as he moved her for the next three count. "We've made a box with our steps. And that is it. Again."

Rachel repeated the moves without much difficulty. "I did it."

"I knew you could. Listen to the music. One, two, three. One, two, three. Ready?"

"I think so."

"One, two, three." And he began moving her in the box step.

After several completed boxes, she looked up. "I'm doing it."

Once she was comfortable with the steps, he said, "Now we're going to turn as we waltz."

Her eyes widened in concern. But she let him lead, and they swirled around the room.

"This is actually easier than the stiff box."

He noticed that the string quartet was transitioning from one waltz to another, allowing him to keep dancing with Rachel without stopping in between pieces.

"I can't believe I'm here dancing with you in front of everyone. Including your father."

"I can't believe Papa is here in English Camp... willingly."

"I think I even saw him smile once."

"Papa? You must be mistaken."

They both laughed, and Charles twirled her around the floor.

"I wish we were alone here."

"Why?"

"I want to kiss you."

Her feet stopped.

He had to do a double step not to land on her feet. He

chuckled. "You stopped dancing." She recovered, and he began leading again.

After an hour at the party, Charles grew nervous when Mr. and Mrs. Thompson aimed for them. He turned to Rachel. "I've had a most enjoyable time with you."

"I don't understand. The party isn't over."

"I think it is for us. Your parents are on their way here."

She turned to see them. "Maybe I can talk them into letting me stay."

Before Rachel could ask, Genevieve took her arm. "Come with me, dear." And Rachel was led away from him.

Charles was a bit nervous under Mr. Thompson's scrutiny but figured the man had something to say to him without Rachel. He braced himself.

Mr. Thompson spoke. "Where do you stand with God?"

"Excuse me, sir?"

"'He that is not with me is against me.' Saint Matthew chapter twelve, verse thirty. Are you with or against God?"

Now he understood. If this man was even going to consider Charles for his daughter, he wanted to know Charles was a Christian. "With, sir. Always with."

Mr. Thompson narrowed his eyes. "What are your intentions toward my daughter?" His question was spoken like an interrogation from his superior.

Charles resisted the urge to squirm. "I love Rachel."

Mr. Thompson seemed more impatient with Charles's answer than upset. "That much is obvious. But what are your *intentions*?"

It was time to lay it all out. Charles filled his lungs. "I intend to prove to you—if you'll permit me—that I am an honorable and trustworthy man, so that one day, when I ask for her hand, you will at least consider me." He had spoken without a breath, so he gulped down air. Well, he'd said it. Mr. Thompson probably wouldn't let him anywhere near his daughter again. But he didn't regret his words. However, he was uncomfortable with the way the older man studied him, like cornered prey.

Finally, Rachel's father spoke. "One day? And how far into the future do you think that will be?"

How was he to know how long it would take this man to accept him? If ever. He could imagine him making Charles do all sorts of difficult things that he hoped Charles would fail at. "I suppose that will be up to you, sir. Tell me what I must do to prove to you that I am an honorable man worthy of your daughter." He had to give the man credit. He at least appeared to be giving it some consideration.

"I suppose if you were to go out in a vicious storm and risk your life climbing down a cliff to save my son, I couldn't ask for much better proof than that."

A stillness captured Charles. He dared not even breathe. Finally he asked, "Are you saying that 'one day' is *today*? That I have your blessing to propose to Rachel?"

Mr. Thompson nodded. "But I wouldn't wait too long. My daughter can be quite impatient."

"Sir, thank you, sir. You won't regret this, sir."

Mr. Thompson's mouth twitched up on one side. "Oh, I'm sure I will a few times in the years to come. But you make my Rachel happy. Next to knowing her place in the Kingdom of Heaven is secure, her happiness is most important to me." After a pause, he continued, "Please don't take her away from here for too long. I couldn't bear it."

Charles pictured Rachel in his social circles back in England. The ladies, if he could call them that, would all hate her for her natural charm and beauty. She was a refreshing contrast. They would try to change her to be more like them. There was nothing wrong with Rachel that needed to be changed.

And the men? They would be like wolves, circling, vying for her attention. Spoken for or not.

England held little appeal for him anymore.

Rachel couldn't bear not knowing what Papa was saying. Probably telling Charles to stay away from her. She *would* have rushed right over and pleaded Charles's case if Genevieve hadn't held her arm firmly, keeping her in place.

Then Charles spoke briefly to his brother and dashed out as though a pack of rabid dogs was after him.

She didn't like that at all and hurried to Papa. "What did you say to him?"

"Men's talk. When it concerns you, you will be informed."

Where Charles was involved, it did concern her. "Will he return to the party?"

"I'm sure he will." Papa had a mischievous glint in his eyes.

She went to the window near the door Charles had escaped through and peered out.

Genevieve came up beside her. "Staring out the window after a man is unbecoming a lady." She took Rachel's arm. "Come away from there."

She hated waiting. Fortunately, she didn't have long to wait.

Returning, Charles came straight toward her, took her hand and led her to the middle of the room, which fell silent. He held out a blue-gemmed ring and lowered to one knee, gazing up at her. "Rachel Thompson, will you do me the great honor of becoming my wife?"

She clasped her hands to her chest and smiled. "I would have to ask Papa."

"I already have. He gave us his blessing."

She turned to Papa for confirmation. When he nodded, she told Charles, "Yes, yes, yes, I'll be your wife."

Everyone cheered.

He slipped the ring on her finger and stood. "This was given to my mother on her eighteenth birthday. I'm the fourth son, and my brothers received the larger jewels for their wives."

"It's beautiful. More than I could have hoped for." She had never had anything so fine.

When he leaned closer, she could tell he meant to kiss her. She put a hand on his chest. A kiss wouldn't be appropriate in public.

Charles pointed up.

Above her head hung mistletoe. She smiled and lowered her hand.

He pressed his lips to hers in a gentle lingering kiss, sweeter than any of the stolen ones they had shared in their clandestine rendezvous. This was the first kiss celebrating their future together.

The room erupted in applause.

Rachel didn't care that everyone was watching. She could stay here forever in her Romeo's embrace.

Real life romance was so much better than any of her books.

* * * * *

REQUEST YOUR FREE BOOKS!

2 FREE INSPIRATIONAL NOVELS
PLUS 2
FREE
MYSTERY GIFTS

Love Inspired®

YES! Please send me 2 FREE Love Inspired® novels and my 2 FREE mystery gifts (gifts are worth about $10). After receiving them, if I don't wish to receive any more books, I can return the shipping statement marked "cancel." If I don't cancel, I will receive 6 brand-new novels every month and be billed just $4.74 per book in the U.S. or $5.24 per book in Canada. That's a savings of at least 21% off the cover price. It's quite a bargain! Shipping and handling is just 50¢ per book in the U.S. and 75¢ per book in Canada.* I understand that accepting the 2 free books and gifts places me under no obligation to buy anything. I can always return a shipment and cancel at any time. Even if I never buy another book, the two free books and gifts are mine to keep forever.

105/305 IDN F49N

Name _____ (PLEASE PRINT) _____

Address _____ Apt. # _____

City _____ State/Prov. _____ Zip/Postal Code _____

Signature (if under 18, a parent or guardian must sign)

Mail to the Harlequin® Reader Service:
IN U.S.A.: P.O. Box 1867, Buffalo, NY 14240-1867
IN CANADA: P.O. Box 609, Fort Erie, Ontario L2A 5X3

**Are you a subscriber to Love Inspired books
and want to receive the larger-print edition?
Call 1-800-873-8635 or visit www.ReaderService.com.**

* Terms and prices subject to change without notice. Prices do not include applicable taxes. Sales tax applicable in N.Y. Canadian residents will be charged applicable taxes. Offer not valid in Quebec. This offer is limited to one order per household. Not valid for current subscribers to Love Inspired books. All orders subject to credit approval. Credit or debit balances in a customer's account(s) may be offset by any other outstanding balance owed by or to the customer. Please allow 4 to 6 weeks for delivery. Offer available while quantities last.

Your Privacy—The Harlequin® Reader Service is committed to protecting your privacy. Our Privacy Policy is available online at www.ReaderService.com or upon request from the Harlequin Reader Service.
We make a portion of our mailing list available to reputable third parties that offer products we believe may interest you. If you prefer that we not exchange your name with third parties, or if you wish to clarify or modify your communication preferences, please visit us at www.ReaderService.com/consumerschoice or write to us at Harlequin Reader Service Preference Service, P.O. Box 9062, Buffalo, NY 14269. Include your complete name and address.

LIDIR13R

REQUEST YOUR FREE BOOKS!

2 FREE RIVETING INSPIRATIONAL NOVELS PLUS 2 FREE MYSTERY GIFTS

YES! Please send me 2 FREE Love Inspired® Suspense novels and my 2 FREE mystery gifts (gifts are worth about $10). After receiving them, if I don't wish to receive any more books, I can return the shipping statement marked "cancel." If I don't cancel, I will receive 4 brand-new novels every month and be billed just $4.74 per book in the U.S. or $5.24 per book in Canada. That's a savings of at least 21% off the cover price. It's quite a bargain! Shipping and handling is just 50¢ per book in the U.S. and 75¢ per book in Canada.* I understand that accepting the 2 free books and gifts places me under no obligation to buy anything. I can always return a shipment and cancel at any time. Even if I never buy another book, the two free books and gifts are mine to keep forever.

123/323 IDN F5AN

Name	(PLEASE PRINT)

Address	Apt. #

City	State/Prov.	Zip/Postal Code

Signature (if under 18, a parent or guardian must sign)

Mail to the Harlequin® Reader Service:
IN U.S.A.: P.O. Box 1867, Buffalo, NY 14240-1867
IN CANADA: P.O. Box 609, Fort Erie, Ontario L2A 5X3

**Are you a current subscriber to Love Inspired Suspense books and want to receive the larger-print edition?
Call 1-800-873-8635 or visit www.ReaderService.com.**

* Terms and prices subject to change without notice. Prices do not include applicable taxes. Sales tax applicable in N.Y. Canadian residents will be charged applicable taxes. Offer not valid in Quebec. This offer is limited to one order per household. Not valid for current subscribers to Love Inspired Suspense books. All orders subject to credit approval. Credit or debit balances in a customer's account(s) may be offset by any other outstanding balance owed by or to the customer. Please allow 4 to 6 weeks for delivery. Offer available while quantities last.

Your Privacy—The Harlequin® Reader Service is committed to protecting your privacy. Our Privacy Policy is available online at www.ReaderService.com or upon request from the Harlequin Reader Service.
We make a portion of our mailing list available to reputable third parties that offer products we believe may interest you. If you prefer that we not exchange your name with third parties, or if you wish to clarify or modify your communication preferences, please visit us at www.ReaderService.com/consumerschoice or write to us at Harlequin Reader Service Preference Service, P.O. Box 9062, Buffalo, NY 14269. Include your complete name and address.

LISDIR13R

REQUEST YOUR FREE BOOKS!

2 FREE INSPIRATIONAL NOVELS
PLUS 2
FREE
MYSTERY GIFTS

Love Inspired.
HISTORICAL
INSPIRATIONAL HISTORICAL ROMANCE

YES! Please send me 2 FREE Love Inspired® Historical novels and my 2 FREE mystery gifts (gifts are worth about $10). After receiving them, if I don't wish to receive any more books, I can return the shipping statement marked "cancel." If I don't cancel, I will receive 4 brand-new novels every month and be billed just $4.74 per book in the U.S. or $5.24 per book in Canada. That's a savings of at least 21% off the cover price. It's quite a bargain! Shipping and handling is just 50¢ per book in the U.S. and 75¢ per book in Canada.* I understand that accepting the 2 free books and gifts places me under no obligation to buy anything. I can always return a shipment and cancel at any time. Even if I never buy another book, the two free books and gifts are mine to keep forever.

102/302 IDN F5CY

Name _____ (PLEASE PRINT) _____

Address _____ Apt. # _____

City _____ State/Prov. _____ Zip/Postal Code _____

Signature (if under 18, a parent or guardian must sign)

Mail to the Harlequin® Reader Service:
IN U.S.A.: P.O. Box 1867, Buffalo, NY 14240-1867
IN CANADA: P.O. Box 609, Fort Erie, Ontario L2A 5X3

Want to try two free books from another series?
Call 1-800-873-8635 or visit www.ReaderService.com.

* Terms and prices subject to change without notice. Prices do not include applicable taxes. Sales tax applicable in N.Y. Canadian residents will be charged applicable taxes. Offer not valid in Quebec. This offer is limited to one order per household. Not valid for current subscribers to Love Inspired Historical books. All orders subject to credit approval. Credit or debit balances in a customer's account(s) may be offset by any other outstanding balance owed by or to the customer. Please allow 4 to 6 weeks for delivery. Offer available while quantities last.

Your Privacy—The Harlequin® Reader Service is committed to protecting your privacy. Our Privacy Policy is available online at www.ReaderService.com or upon request from the Harlequin Reader Service.

We make a portion of our mailing list available to reputable third parties that offer products we believe may interest you. If you prefer that we not exchange your name with third parties, or if you wish to clarify or modify your communication preferences, please visit us at www.ReaderService.com/consumerchoice or write to us at Harlequin Reader Service Preference Service, P.O. Box 9062, Buffalo, NY 14269. Include your complete name and address.

LIHDIR13R

ReaderService.com

Manage your account online!

- Review your order history
- Manage your payments
- Update your address

*We've designed
the Harlequin® Reader Service
website just for you.*

Enjoy all the features!

- Reader excerpts from any series
- Respond to mailings and
  special monthly offers
- Discover new series available to you
- Browse the Bonus Bucks catalog
- Share your feedback

Visit us at:

ReaderService.com